THE EVIL GENIUS

A Domestic Story

BY

WILKIE COLLINS

IN THREE VOLUMES

VOL. II

London

CHATTO AND WINDUS, PICCADILLY

1886

CONTENTS OF VOL. II.

CONTENTS.

FOURTH BOOK.

THE EVIL GENIUS.

SECOND BOOK.

19

CHAPTER XV.

As the year advanced, the servants at Mount Morven remarked that the weeks seemed to follow each other more slowly than usual. In the higher regions of the house, the same impression was prevalent ; but the sense of dulness among the gentlefolks submitted to circumstances in silence.

If the question had been asked in past days : Who is the brightest and happiest member of the family? Everybody would have said : Kitty. If the question had been asked at the present time, differences

19—2

of opinion might have suggested different answers—but the whole household would have refrained without hesitation from mentioning the child's name.

Since Sydney Westerfield's departure Kitty had never held up her head.

Time quieted the child's first vehement outbreaks of distress under the loss of the companion whom she had so dearly loved. Delicate management, gently yet resolutely applied, held the faithful little creature in check, when she tried to discover the cause of her governess's banishment from the house. She made no more complaints; she asked no more embarrassing questions —but it was miserably plain to everybody about her that she failed to recover her spirits. She was willing to learn her lessons (not under another governess) when her mother was able to attend to her : she played with her toys, and went out riding on her pony. But the delightful gaiety of other days was gone ; the shrill laughter that once rang through the house was heard no more. Kitty had become a quiet child ; and, worse still, a child who seemed to be easily tired.

The doctor was consulted.

He was a man skilled in the sound medical practice that learns its lessons without books — bedside practice. His opinion declared that the child's vital power was seriously lowered. " Some cause is at work here," he said to the mother, " which I don't understand. Can you help me?" Mrs. Linley helped him without hesitation. " My little daughter dearly loved her governess ; and her governess has been obliged to leave us." That was her reply. The doctor wanted to hear no more ; he at once advised that Kitty should be taken to the sea-side, and that everything which might remind her of the absent friend—books, presents, even articles of clothing likely to revive old associations—should be left at home. A new life, in new air. When pen, ink and paper were offered to him, that was the doctor's prescription.

Mrs. Linley consulted her husband on the choice of the sea-side place to which the child should be removed.

The blank which Sydney's departure left in the life of the household was felt by the master and mistress of Mount Morven —and felt, unhappily, without any open avowal on either side of what was passing in their minds. In this way, the governess became a forbidden subject between them; the husband waited for the wife to set the example of approaching it, and the wife waited for the husband. The trial of temper produced by this state of hesitation, and by the secret doubts which it encouraged, led insensibly to a certain estrangement—which Linley in particular was morbidly unwilling to acknowledge. If, when the dinner hour brought them together, he was silent and dull in his wife's presence, he attributed it to anxiety on the subject of his brother—then absent on a critical business-errand in London. If he sometimes left the house the first thing in the morning, and only returned at night, it was because the management of the model farm had become one of his duties, in Randal's absence. Mrs. Linley made no attempt to dispute this view of the altered circumstances in home-life—but she submitted with a mind ill at ease. Secretly fearing that Linley was suffering under Miss Westerfield's absence, she allowed herself to hope that Kitty's father would see a necessity, in his own case, for change of scene, and would accompany them to the sea-side.

"Won't you come with us, Herbert?" she suggested, when they had both agreed on the choice of a place.

His temper was in a state of constant irritation. Without meaning it, he answered her harmless question sharply.

"How can I go away with you, when we are losing by the farm, and when there is nobody to check the ruinous expenses but myself?"

Mrs. Linley's thoughts naturally turned to Randal's prolonged absence. "What can be keeping him all this time in London?" she said.

Linley's failing patience suffered a severe trial.

"Don't you know," he broke out, "that I have inherited my poor mother's property in England, saddled with a law-suit?

Have you never heard of delays and disappointments, and quibbles and false pretences, encountered by unfortunate wretches like me who are obliged to go to law? God only knows when Randal will be free to return, or what bad news he may bring with him when he does come back."

"You have many anxieties, Herbert; and I ought to have remembered them."

That gentle answer touched him. He made the best apology in his power, he said his nerves were out of order, and asked her to excuse him if he had spoken roughly. There was no unfriendly feeling on either side ; and yet there was something wanting in the reconciliation. Mrs. Linley left her husband, shaken by a conflict of feelings. At one moment she felt angry with him ; at another she felt angry with herself.

With the best intentions (as usual) Mrs.

Presty made mischief, nevertheless. Observing that her daughter was in tears, and feeling sincerely distressed by the discovery, she was eager to administer consolation. " Make your mind easy, my dear, if you have any doubt about Herbert's movements when he is away from home. I followed him myself the day before yesterday when he went out. A long walk for an old woman—but I can assure you that he does really go to the farm."

Implicitly trusting her husband — and rightly trusting him—Linley's wife replied by a look which Mrs. Presty received in silent indignation. She summoned her dignity and marched out of the room.

Five minutes afterwards, Mrs. Linley received an intimation that her mother was seriously offended, in the form of a little note :

" I find that my maternal interest in

your welfare, and my devoted efforts to serve you, are only rewarded with furious looks. The less we see of each other the better. Permit me to thank you for your invitation, and to decline accompanying you when you leave Mount Morven to-morrow."

Mrs. Linley answered the note in person. The next day Kitty's grandmother—ripe for more mischief on the next favourable occasion—altered her mind, and thoroughly enjoyed her journey to the sea-side.

CHAPTER XVI.

THE CHILD.

DURING the first week there was an improvement in the child's health, which justified the doctor's hopeful anticipations. Mrs. Linley wrote cheerfully to her husband; and the better nature of Mrs. Linley's mother seemed, by some inscrutable process, to thrive morally under the encouraging influences of the sea air. It may be a bold thing to say, but it is surely true that our virtues depend greatly on the state of our health.

During the second week, the reports sent to Mount Morven were less encouraging.

The improvement in Kitty was maintained; but it made no further progress.

The lapse of the third week brought with it depressing results. There could be no doubt now that the child was losing ground. Bitterly disappointed, Mrs. Linley wrote to her medical adviser, describing the symptoms, and asking for instructions. The doctor wrote back: " Find out where your supply of drinking water comes from. If from a well, let me know how it is situated. Answer by telegraph." The reply arrived : " A well near the parish church." The doctor's advice ran back along the wires : " Come home instantly."

They returned the same day—and they returned too late.

Kitty's first night at home was wakeful and restless; her little hands felt feverish, and she was tormented by perpetual thirst. The good doctor still spoke hopefully;

attributing the symptoms to fatigue after the journey. But, as the days followed each other, his medical visits were paid at shorter intervals. The mother noticed that his pleasant face became grave and anxious; and implored him to tell her the truth. The truth was told in two dreadful words : " Typhoid Fever."

A day or two later, the doctor spoke privately with Mr. Linley. The child's debilitated condition—that lowered state of the vital power which he had observed when Kitty's case was first submitted to him—placed a terrible obstacle in the way of successful resistance to the advance of the disease. " Say nothing to Mrs. Linley just yet. There is no absolute danger so far, unless delirium sets in." " Do you think it likely?" Linley asked. The doctor shook his head, and said, " God knows."

On the next evening but one, the fatal

symptom showed itself. There was nothing violent in the delirium. Unconscious of past events in the family life, the poor child supposed that her governess was living in the house as usual. She piteously wondered why Sydney remained downstairs in the schoolroom. "Oh, don't keep her away from me! I want Syd! I want Syd!" That was her one cry. When exhaustion silenced her, they hoped that the sad delusion was at an end. No! As the slow fire of the fever flamed up again, the same words were on the child's lips, the same fond hope was in her sinking heart.

The doctor led Mrs. Linley out of the room. "Is this the governess?" he asked.

"Yes!"

"Is she within easy reach?"

"She is employed in the family of a friend of ours, living five miles away from us."

" Send for her instantly !"

Mrs. Linley looked at him with a wildly-mingled expression of hope and fear.   She was not thinking of herself—she was not even thinking, for that one moment, of the child.   What would her husband say, if she (who had extorted his promise never to see the governess again) brought Sydney Westerfield back to the house ?

The doctor spoke to her more strongly still.

" I don't presume to inquire into your private reasons for hesitating to follow my advice," he said ; " but I am bound to tell you the truth.   My poor little patient is in serious danger—every hour of delay is an hour gained by death.   Bring that lady to the bedside as fast as a carriage can fetch her, and let us see the result.   If Kitty recognises her governess—there, I tell you plainly, is the one chance of saving the child's life."

Mrs. Linley's resolution flashed on him in her weary eyes—the eyes which, by day and night alike, had known so little rest. She rang for her maid. " Tell your master I want to speak to him."

The woman answered : " My master has gone out."

The doctor watched the mother's face. No sign of hesitation appeared in it—the one thought in her mind now was the thought of the child. She called the maid back.

" Order the carriage."

" At what time do you want it, ma'am ?"

" At once!"

CHAPTER XVII.

THE HUSBAND.

MRS. LINLEY's first impulse in ordering the carriage was to use it herself. One look at the child reminded her that her freedom of action began and ended at the bedside. More than an hour must elapse before Sydney Westerfield could be brought back to Mount Morven; the bare thought of what might happen in that interval, if she was absent, filled the mother with horror. She wrote to Mrs. MacEdwin, and sent her maid with the letter.

Of the result of this proceeding it was not possible to entertain a doubt.

Sydney's love for Kitty would hesitate at no sacrifice; and Mrs. MacEdwin's conduct had already answered for her. She had received the governess with the utmost kindness, and she had generously and delicately refrained from asking any questions. But one person at Mount Morven thought it necessary to investigate the motives under which she had acted. Mrs. Presty's inquiring mind arrived at discoveries; and Mrs. Presty's sense of duty communicated them to her daughter.

"There can be no sort of doubt, Catherine, that our good friend and neighbour has heard, probably from the servants, of what has happened; and (having her husband to consider—men are so weak!) has drawn her own conclusions. If she trusts our fascinating governess, it's because she knows that Miss Westerfield's affections are left behind

20—2

her in this house.   Does my explanation
., satisfy you?"

Mrs. Linley said: "Never let me hear it
again!"

And Mrs. Presty answered: "How very
ungrateful!"

The dreary interval of expectation, after
the departure of the carriage, was brightened
by a domestic event.

Thinking it possible that Mrs. Presty
might know why her husband had left the
house, Mrs. Linley sent to ask for information.   The message in reply informed her
that Linley had received a telegram announcing Randal's return from London.
He had gone to the railway station to meet
his brother.

Before she went downstairs to welcome
Randal, Mrs. Linley paused to consider her
situation.   The one alternative before her
was to acknowledge at the earliest oppor-

tunity that she had assumed the serious responsibility of sending for Sydney Westerfield. For the first time in her life, Catherine Linley found herself planning beforehand what she would say in speaking to her husband.

A second message interrupted her, announcing that the two brothers had just arrived. She joined them immediately in the drawing-room.

Linley was sitting in a corner by himself. The dreadful discovery that the child's life (by the doctor's confession) was in danger had completely overwhelmed him: he never even lifted his head when his wife opened the door. Randal and Mrs. Presty were talking together. The old lady's insatiable curiosity was eager for news from London : she wanted to know how Randal had amused himself when he was not attending to business.

He was grieving for Kitty; and he was looking sadly at his brother. "I don't remember," he answered absently. Other women might have discovered that they had chosen their time badly. Mrs. Presty, with the best possible intentions, remonstrated.

"Really, Randal, you must rouse yourself. Surely you can tell us something. Did you meet with any agreeable people, while you were away?"

"I met one person who interested me," he said, with weary resignation.

Mrs. Presty smiled. "A woman, of course!"

"A man," Randal answered; "a guest like myself at a club dinner."

"Who is he?"

"Captain Bennydeck."

"In the army?"

"No: formerly in the navy."

"And you and he had a long talk together?"

Randal's tones began to betray irritation. "No," he said; "the Captain went away early."

Mrs. Presty's vigorous intellect discovered an improbability here. "Then how came you to feel interested in him?" she objected.

Even Randal's patience gave way. "I can't account for it," he said, sharply. "I only know I took a liking to Captain Bennydeck." He left Mrs. Presty, and sat down by his brother. "You know I feel for you," he said, taking Linley's hand. "Try to hope."

The bitterness of the father's despair broke out in his answer. "I can bear other troubles, Randal, as well as most men. This affliction revolts me. There's something so horribly unnatural in the child being threatened by death, while the parents (who should die first) are alive and well—" He checked himself. "I had better say no more, I shall only shock you."

The misery in his face wrung the faithful heart of his wife. She forgot the conciliatory expressions which she had prepared herself to use. "Hope, my dear, as Randal tells you," she said, "because there *is* hope."

His face flushed, his dim eyes brightened. "Has the doctor said it?" he asked.

"Yes."

"Why haven't I been told of it before?"

"When I sent for you, I heard that you had gone out."

The explanation passed by him unnoticed—perhaps even unheard. "Tell me what the doctor said," he insisted; "I want it exactly, word for word."

She obeyed him to the letter.

The sinister change in his face, as the narrative proceeded, was observed by both the other persons present, as well as by his wife. She waited for a kind word of encouragement. He only said coldly: "What have you done?"

Speaking coldly on her side, she answered: "I have sent the carriage to fetch Miss Westerfield."

There was a pause. Mrs. Presty whispered to Randal: "I knew she would come back again! The Evil Genius of the family —that's what I call Miss Westerfield. The name exactly fits her!"

The idea in Randal's mind was that the name exactly fitted Mrs. Presty. He made no reply: his eyes rested in sympathy on his sister-in-law. She saw, and felt, his kindness at a time when kindness was doubly precious. Her tones trembled a little as she spoke to her silent husband.

"Don't you approve of what I have done, Herbert?"

His nerves were shattered by grief and suspense ; but he made an effort this time to speak gently. " How can I say that," he replied, " if the poor child's life depends on Miss Westerfield? I ask one favour— give me time to leave the house before she comes here."

Mrs. Linley looked at him in amazement.

Her mother touched her arm ; Randal tried by a sign to warn her to be careful. Their calmer minds had seen what the wife's agitation had prevented her from discovering. In Linley's position, the return of the governess was a trial to his self-control which he had every reason to dread : his look, his voice, his manner proclaimed it to persons capable of quietly observing him. He had struggled against his guilty passion—at what sacrifice of his own feelings no one knew but himself—and here was the temptation, at the very time when he was honourably resisting it, brought back to him by his wife! Her motive did unquestionably excuse, perhaps even sanction, what she had done; but this was an estimate of her conduct which commended itself to others. From his point of view— motive or no motive—he saw the old struggle against himself in danger of being renewed; he felt the ground that he had gained slipping from under him already.

In spite of the well-meant efforts made by her relatives to prevent it, Mrs. Linley committed the very error which it was most important that she should avoid. She justified herself, instead of leaving it to events to justify her. " Miss Westerfield comes here," she argued, " on an errand that is beyond reproach—an errand of mercy. Why should you leave the house ?"

"In justice to you," Linley answered.

Mrs. Presty could restrain herself no longer. "Drop it, Catherine!" she said in a whisper.

Catherine refused to drop it; Linley's short and sharp reply had irritated her. "After my experience," she persisted, "have I no reason to trust you?"

"It is part of your experience," he reminded her, "that I promised not to see Miss Westerfield again."

"Own it at once!" she broke out, provoked beyond endurance; "though I may be willing to trust you—you are afraid to trust yourself."

Unlucky Mrs. Presty interfered again. "Don't listen to her, Herbert. Keep out of harm's way, and you keep right."

She patted him on the shoulder, as if she had been giving good advice to a boy. He expressed his sense of his mother-in-

♥'s friendly offices in language which ♥onished her.

" Hold your tongue!"

" Do you hear that?" Mrs. Presty asked, ♥ppealing indignantly to her daughter.

Linley took his hat. " At what time do you expect Miss Westerfield to arrive?" he said to his wife.

She looked at the clock on the mantel-piece. " Before the half-hour strikes. Don't be alarmed," she added, with an air of ironical sympathy; " you will have time to make your escape."

He advanced to the door, and looked at her.

" One thing I beg you will remember," he said. " Every half-hour while I am away (I am going to the farm) you are to send and let me know how Kitty is—and especially if Miss Westerfield justifies the experiment which the doctor has advised us to try."

Having given those instructions he went out.

The sofa was near Mrs. Linley. She sank on it, overpowered by the utter destruction of the hopes that she had founded on the separation of Herbert and the governess. Sydney Westerfield was still in possession of her husband's heart!

Her mother was surely the right person to say a word of comfort to her. Randal made the suggestion—with the worst possible result. Mrs. Presty had not forgotten that she had been told—at her age, in her position as the widow of a Cabinet Minister —to hold her tongue. "Your brother has insulted me," she said to Randal. He was weak enough to attempt to make an explanation. "I was speaking of my brother's wife," he said. "Your brother's wife has allowed me to be insulted." Having received that reply Randal could only wonder.

This woman went to church every Sunday! and kept a New Testament, bound in excellent taste, on her toilette-table. The occasion suggested reflection on the system which produces average Christians at the present time. Nothing more was said by Mrs. Presty; Mrs. Linley remained absorbed in her own bitter thoughts. In silence they waited for the return of the carriage, and the appearance of the governess.

CHAPTER XVIII.

THE NURSEMAID.

PALE, worn, haggard with anxiety, Sydney Westerfield entered the room, and looked once more on the faces which she had resigned herself never to see again. She appeared to be hardly conscious of the kind reception which did its best to set her at her ease.

" Am I in time?" were the first words that escaped her on entering the room. Reassured by the answer, she turned back to the door ; eager to hurry upstairs to Kitty's bedside.

Mrs. Linley's gentle hand detained her.

The doctor had left certain instructions,

ning the mother to guard against any
ccident that might remind Kitty of the day
on which Sydney had left her. At the
time of that bitter parting, the child had
seen her governess in the same walking-
dress which she wore now. Mrs. Linley
removed the hat and cloak, and laid them
on a chair.

" There is one other precaution which
we must observe," she said ; " I must ask
you to wait in my room until I find that
you may show yourself safely. Now come
with me."

Mrs. Presty followed them, and begged
earnestly for leave to wait the result of the
momentous experiment, at the door of
Kitty's bedroom. Her self-asserting manner had vanished; she was quiet, she was
even humble. While the last chance for
the child's life was fast becoming a matter
of minutes only, the grandmother's better

nature showed itself on the surface. Randal opened the door for them as the three went out together. He was in that state of maddening anxiety about his poor little niece, in which men of his imaginative temperament become morbid, and say strangely inappropriate things. In the same breath with which he implored his sister-in-law to let him hear what had happened, without an instant of delay, he startled Mrs. Presty by one of his familiar remarks on the inconsistencies in her character. " You disagreeable old woman," he whispered, as she passed him, "you have got a heart after all."

Left alone, he was never for one moment in repose, while the slow minutes followed each other in the silent house.

He walked about the room, he listened at the door, he arranged and disarranged the furniture. When the nursemaid dended from the upper regions with her mistress's message for him, he ran out to meet her; saw the good news in her smiling face; and, for the first and last time in his life, kissed one of his brother's female servants. Susan—a well-bred young person, thoroughly capable in ordinary cases of saying "For shame, sir!" and looking as if she expected to feel an arm round her waist next—trembled with terror under that astounding salute. Her master's brother, a pattern of propriety up to that time, a man declared by her fellow-servants to be incapable of kissing a woman unless she had a right to insist on it in the licensed character of his wife, had evidently taken leave of his senses. Would he bite her next? No: he only looked confused, and said (how very extraordinary!) that he would never do it again. Susan gave her message gravely.

21—2

Here was an unintelligible man; she felt the necessity of being careful in her choice of words.

"Miss Kitty stared at Miss Westerfield —only for a moment, sir—as if she didn't quite understand, and then knew her again directly. The doctor has just called. He drew up the blind to let the light in, and he looked, and he says, ' Only be careful '——" Tender-hearted Susan broke down, and began to cry. "I can't help it, sir; we are all so fond of Miss Kitty, and we are so happy. ' Only be careful ' (those were the exact words, if you please), ' and I answer for her life.'—Oh, dear! what have I said to make him run away from me?"

Randal had left her abruptly, and had shut himself into the drawing-room. Susan's experience of men had not yet informed her that a true Englishman is ashamed to be seen (especially by his inferiors) with the tears in his eyes.

- He had barely succeeded in composing himself, when another servant appeared— this time a man—with something to say to him.

"I don't knew whether I have done right, sir," Malcolm began. "There's a stranger downstairs among the tourists who are looking at the rooms and the pictures. He said he knew you. And he asked if you were not related to the gentleman who allowed travellers to see his interesting old house."

"Well?"

"Well, sir, I said Yes. And then he wanted to know if you happened to be here at the present time."

Randal cut the man's story short. "And you said Yes again, and he gave you his card. Let me look at it."

Malcolm produced the card, and instantly received instructions to show the gentleman up. The name recalled the dinner at the London club—Captain Bennydeck.

CHAPTER XIX.

THE CAPTAIN.

THE fair complexion of the Captain's youthful days had been darkened by exposure to
hard weather and extreme climates. His
smooth face of twenty years since was scored
by the tell-tale marks of care; his dark
beard was beginning to present variety of
colour by means of streaks of grey; and his
hair was in course of undisguised retreat
from his strong broad forehead. Not rising
above the middle height, the Captain's spare
figure was well preserved. It revealed
power and activity, severely tested perhaps
at some former time, but capable even yet

of endurance under trial. Although he looked older than his age, he was still personally speaking an attractive man. In repose, his eyes were by habit sad, and a little weary in their expression. They only caught a brighter light when he smiled. At such times, helped by this change and by his simple earnest manner, they recommended him to his fellow-creatures before he opened his lips. Men and women taking shelter with him, for instance, from the rain, found the temptation to talk with Captain Bennydeck irresistible ; and, when the weather cleared, they mostly carried away with them the same favourable impression: " One would like to meet with that gentleman again."

Randal's first words of welcome relieved the Captain of certain modest doubts of his reception, which appeared to trouble him when he entered the room. " I am glad to find you remember me as kindly as I remember you." Those were his first words when he and Randal shook hands.

"You might have felt sure of that," Randal said.

The Captain's modesty still doubted. "You see, the circumstances were a little against me. We met at a dull dinner, among wearisome worldly men, full of boastful talk about themselves. It was all, ' I did this ' and ' I said that '—and the gentlemen who were present had always been right; and the gentlemen who were absent had always been wrong. And, oh, dear, when they came to politics, how they bragged about what they would have done if they had only been at the head of the Government ; and how cruelly hard to please they were in the matter of wine! Do you remember recommending me to spend my next holiday in Scotland?"

"Perfectly. My advice was selfish—it really meant that I wanted to see you again."

"And you have your wish, at your brother's house! The guidebook did it. First, I saw your family name. Then, I read on and discovered that there were pictures at Mount Morven, and that strangers were allowed to see them. I like pictures. And here I am."

This allusion to the house naturally reminded Randal of the master. "I wish I could introduce you to my brother and his wife," he said. "Unhappily their only child is ill——"

Captain Bennydeck started to his feet. "I am ashamed of having intruded on you," he began. His new friend pressed him back into his chair without ceremony. "On the contrary, you have arrived at the best of all possible times—the time when our suspense is at an end. The doctor has just told us that his poor little patient is out of danger. You may imagine how happy we are."

"And how grateful to God!" The Captain said those words in tones that trembled—speaking to himself.

Randal was conscious of feeling a momentary embarrassment. The character of his visitor had presented itself in a new light. Captain Bennydeck looked at him—understood him—and returned to the subject of his travels.

" Do you remember your holiday time when you were a boy, and when you had to go back to school?" he asked with a smile. " My mind is in much the same state at leaving Scotland, and going back to my work in London. I hardly know which I admire most—your beautiful country or the people who inhabit it. I have had

some pleasant talk with your poorer neighbours; the one improvement I could wish
for among them is a keener sense of their
religious duties."

This was an objection, new in Randal's
experience of travellers in general.

" Our Highlanders have noble qualities,"
he said. " If you knew them as well as I
do, you would find a true sense of religion
among them ; not presenting itself, however, to strangers as strongly—I had almost
said as aggressively — as the devotional
feeling of the Lowland Scotch. Different
races, different temperaments."

" And all," the Captain added, gravely
and gently, " with souls to be saved. If I
sent to these poor people some copies of
the New Testament, translated into their
own language, would my gift be accepted?"

Strongly interested, by this time, in
studying Captain Bennydeck's character

on the side of it which was new to him, Randal owned that he observed with surprise the interest which his friend felt in perfect strangers. The Captain seemed to wonder why this impression should have been produced by what he had just said.

"I only try," he answered, "to do what good I can, wherever I go."

"Your life must be a happy one," Randal said.

Captain Bennydeck's head drooped. The shadows that attend on the gloom of melancholy remembrance showed their darkening presence on his face. Briefly, almost sternly, he set Randal right.

"No, sir."

"Forgive me," the younger man pleaded, "if I have spoken thoughtlessly."

"You have mistaken me," the Captain explained; "and it is my fault. My life is an atonement for the sins of my youth.

I have reached my fortieth year—and that one purpose is before me for the rest of my days.　Sufferings and dangers which but few men undergo awakened my conscience. My last exercise of the duties of my profession associated me with an expedition to the Polar Seas.　Our ship was crushed in the ice.　Our march to the nearest regions inhabited by humanity was a hopeless struggle of starving men, rotten with scurvy, against the merciless forces of Nature.　One by one my comrades dropped and died.　Out of twenty men, there were three left with a last flicker in them of the vital flame, when the party of rescue found us.　One of the three died on the homeward voyage.　One lived to reach his native place, and to sink to rest with his wife and children round his bed.　The last man left, out of that band of martyrs to a hopeless cause, lives to be worthier

God's mercy—and tries to make God's creatures better and happier in this world, and worthier of the world that is to come."

Randal's generous nature felt the appeal that had been made to it. " Will you let me take your hand, Captain?" he said.

They clasped hands in silence.

Captain Bennydeck was the first to speak again. That modest distrust of himself, which a man essentially noble and brave is generally the readiest of men to feel, seemed to be troubling him once more—just as it had troubled him when he first found himself in Randal's presence.

" I hope you won't think me vain," he resumed; " I seldom say so much about myself as I have said to you."

" I only wish you would say more," Randal rejoined. " Can't you put off your return to London for a day or two?"

The thing was not to be done. Duties

which it was impossible to trifle with called
the Captain back. "It's quite likely," he
said, alluding pleasantly to the impression
which he had produced in speaking of the
Highlanders, "that I shall find more
strangers to interest me in the great city."

"Are they always strangers?" Randal
asked. "Have you never met by accident
with persons whom you may once have
known?"

"Never—yet. But it may happen on my
return."

"In what way?"

"In this way. I have been in search of a
poor girl who has lost both her parents:
she has, I fear, been left helpless at the
mercy of the world. Her father was an old
friend of mine—once an officer in the
Navy, like myself. The agent whom I
formerly employed (without success) to
trace her, writes me word that he has reason

to believe she has obtained a situation as pupil-teacher at a school in the suburbs of London; and I am going back (among other things) to try if I can follow the clue myself. Good-bye, my friend. I am heartily sorry to go!"

"Life is made up of partings," Randal answered.

"And of meetings," the Captain wisely reminded him. "When you are in London, you will always hear of me at the club."

Heartily reciprocating his good wishes, Randal attended Captain Bennydeck to the door. On the way back to the drawing-room, he found his mind dwelling, rather to his surprise, on the Captain's contemplated search for the lost girl.

Was the good man likely to find her? It seemed useless enough to inquire—and yet

Randal asked himself the question. Her father had been described as an officer in the Navy. Well, and what did that matter? Inclined to laugh at his own idle curiosity, he was suddenly struck by a new idea. What had his brother told him of Miss Westerfield? *She* was the daughter of an officer in the Navy; *she* had been pupil-teacher at a school. Was it really possible that Sydney Westerfield could be the person whom Captain Bennydeck was attempting to trace? Randal threw up the window which overlooked the drive in front of the house. Too late! The carriage which had brought the Captain to Mount Morven was no longer in sight.

The one other course that he could take was to mention Captain Bennydeck's name to Sydney, and be guided by the result.

As he approached the bell, determining to

send a message upstairs, he heard the door opened behind him. Mrs. Presty had entered the drawing-room, with a purpose (as it seemed) in which Randal was concerned.

CHAPTER XX.

THE MOTHER-IN-LAW.

STRONG as the impression was which Captain Bennydeck had produced on Randal, Mrs. Presty's first words dismissed it from his mind. She asked him if he had any message for his brother.

Randal instantly looked at the clock. "Has Catherine not sent to the farm, yet?" he asked in astonishment.

Mrs. Presty's mind seemed to be absorbed in her daughter. "Ah, poor Catherine! Worn out with anxiety and watching at Kitty's bedside. Night after night without any sleep; night after night tortured by suspense. As usual, she can depend on her old mother for sympathy. I have taken all her household duties on myself, till she is in better health."

Randal tried again. "Mrs. Presty, am I to understand (after the plain directions Herbert gave) that no messenger has been sent to the farm?"

Mrs. Presty held her venerable head higher than ever, when Randal pronounced his brother's name. "I see no necessity for being in a hurry," she answered stiffly, "after the brutal manner in which Herbert has behaved to me. Put yourself in my place—and imagine what you would feel if you were told to hold your tongue."

Randal wasted no more time on ears that were deaf to remonstrance. Feeling the serious necessity of interfering to some good purpose, he asked where he might find his sister-in-law.

" I have taken Catherine into the garden,"
Mrs. Presty announced. " The doctor himself suggested—no, I may say, ordered it.
He is afraid that *she* may fall ill next, poor
soul, if she doesn't get air and exercise."

In Mrs. Linley's own interests, Randal
resolved on advising her to write to her
husband by the messenger; explaining that
she was not to blame for the inexcusable
delay which had already taken place.
Without a word more to Mrs. Presty, he
hastened out of the room. That invete-
rately distrustful woman called him back.
She desired to know where he was going,
and why he was in a hurry.

" I am going to the garden," Randal
answered.

" To speak to Catherine?"

" Yes."

" Needless trouble, my dear Randal. She
will be back in a quarter of an hour, and

she will pass through this room on her way upstairs."

Another quarter of an hour was a matter of no importance to Mrs. Presty! Randal took his own way—the way into the garden.

His silence and his determination to join his sister-in-law roused Mrs. Presty's ready suspicions; she concluded that he was bent on making mischief between her daughter and herself. The one thing to do in this case was to follow him instantly. The active old lady trotted out of the room, strongly inclined to think that the Evil Genius of the family might be Randal Linley, after all!

They had both taken the shortest way to the garden; that is to say, the way through the library, which communicated at its farthest end with the corridor and the vaulted flight of stairs leading directly out

of the house. Of the two doors in the
drawing-room, one, on the left, led to the
grand staircase and the hall; the other, on
the right, opened on the back-stairs, and on
a side-entrance to the house, used by the
family when they were pressed for time, as
well as by the servants.

The drawing-room had not been empty
more than a few minutes when the door on
the right was suddenly opened. Herbert
Linley entered with hurried, uncertain steps.
He took the chair that was nearest to him,
and dropped into it like a man overpowered
by agitation or fatigue.

He had ridden from the farm at headlong
speed, terrified by the unexplained delay in
the arrival of the messenger from home.
Unable any longer to suffer the torment
of unrelieved suspense, he had returned to
make inquiry at the house. As he inter-
preted the otherwise inexplicable neglect of

his instructions, the last chance of saving the child's life had failed, and his wife had been afraid to tell him the dreadful truth.

After an interval, he rose, and went into the library.

It was empty, like the drawing-room. The bell was close by him. He lifted his hand to ring it—and drew back. As brave a man as ever lived, he knew what fear was now. The father's courage failed him before the prospect of summoning a servant, and hearing, for all he knew to the contrary, that his child was dead.

How long he stood there, alone and irresolute, he never remembered when he thought of it in after days. All he knew was that there came a time when a sound in the drawing-room attracted his attention. It was nothing more important than the opening of a door.

The sound came from that side of the

room which was nearest to the grand staircase—and therefore nearest also to the hall,
in one direction, and to the bed-chambers
in the other.

Some person had entered the room.
Whether it was one of the family, or one
of the servants, he would hear in either
case what had happened in his absence.
He parted the curtains over the library
entrance, and looked through.

The person was a woman. She stood
with her back turned towards the library,
lifting a cloak off a chair. As she shook
the cloak out before putting it on, she
changed her position. He saw the face,
never to be forgotten by him to the last
day of his life. He saw Sydney Westerfield.

CHAPTER XXI.

THE GOVERNESS.

LINLEY had one instant left, in which he might have drawn back into the library in time to escape Sydney's notice. He was incapable of the effort of will. Grief and suspense had deprived him of that elastic readiness of mind which springs at once from thought to action. For a moment he hesitated. In that moment she looked up and saw him.

With a faint cry of alarm she let the cloak drop from her hands. As helpless as he was, as silent as he was, she stood rooted to the spot.

He tried to control himself. Hardly knowing what he said, he made commonplace excuses, as if he had been a stranger: "I am sorry to have startled you; I had no idea of finding you in this room."

Sydney pointed to her cloak on the floor, and to her hat on a chair near it. Understanding the necessity which had brought her into the room, he did his best to reconcile her to the meeting that had followed.

"It's a relief to me to have seen you," he said, "before you leave us."

A relief to him to see her! Why? How? What did that strange word mean, addressed to *her?* She roused herself, and put the question to him.

"It's surely better for me," he answered, "to hear the miserable news from you than from a servant."

"What miserable news?" she asked, still as perplexed as ever.

He could preserve his self-control no longer; the misery in him forced its way outward at last. The convulsive struggles for breath which burst from a man in tears shook him from head to foot.

"My poor little darling!" he gasped. "My only child!"

All that was embarrassing in her position passed from Sydney's mind in an instant. She stepped close up to him; she laid her hand gently and fearlessly on his arm. "Oh, Mr. Linley, what dreadful mistake is this?"

His dim eyes rested on her with a piteous expression of doubt. He heard her—and he was afraid to believe her. She was too deeply distressed, too full of the truest pity for him, to wait and think before she spoke. "Yes! yes!" she cried, under the impulse of the moment. "The dear child knew me again, the moment I spoke to

her. Kitty's recovery is only a matter of
time."

He staggered back—with a livid change
in his face startling to see. The mischief
done by Mrs. Presty's sense of injury
had led already to serious results. If the
thought in Linley, at that moment, had
shaped itself into words, he would have
said, " And Catherine never told me of it?"
How bitterly he thought of the woman who
had left him in suspense—how gratefully
he felt towards the woman who had lightened his heart of the heaviest burden ever
laid on it!

Innocent of all suspicion of the feeling
that she had aroused, Sydney blamed her
own want of discretion as the one cause of
the change that she perceived in him.
" How thoughtless, how cruel of me," she
said, " not to have been more careful in telling you the good news! Pray forgive me."

" You thoughtless ! you cruel !" At the
bare idea of her speaking in that way of
herself, his sense of what he owed to her
defied all restraint. He seized her hands
and covered them with grateful kisses.
" Dear Sydney !—dear, good Sydney !"

She drew back from him; not abruptly,
not as if she felt offended. Her fine per-
ception penetrated the meaning of those
harmless kisses—the uncontrollable out-
burst of a sense of relief beyond the reach
of expression in words. But she changed
the subject. Mrs. Linley (she told him)
had kindly ordered fresh horses to be put
to the carriage, so that she might go back
to her duties if the doctor sanctioned it.

She turned away to take up her cloak.
Linley stopped her. " You can't leave
Kitty," he said positively.

A faint smile brightened her face for a
moment. " Kitty has fallen asleep—such

a sweet, peaceful sleep! I don't think I should have left her but for that. The maid is watching at the bedside, and Mrs. Linley is only away for a little while."

"Wait a few minutes," he pleaded, "it's so long since we have seen each other."

The tone in which he spoke warned her to persist in leaving him while her resolution remained firm. "I had arranged with Mrs. MacEdwin," she began, "if all went well——"

"Speak of yourself," he interposed. "Tell me if you are happy."

She let this pass without a reply. "The doctor sees no harm," she went on, "in my being away for a few hours. Mrs. Mac-Edwin has offered to send me here in the evening, so that I can sleep in Kitty's room."

"You don't look well, Sydney. You are pale and worn—you are not happy."

She began to tremble. For the second time, she turned away to take up her cloak. For the second time, he stopped her.

"Not just yet," he said. "You don't know how it distresses me to see you so sadly changed. I remember the time when you were the happiest creature living. Do you remember it too?"

"Don't ask me!" was all she could say.

He sighed as he looked at her. "It's dreadful to think of your young life, that ought to be so bright, wasting and withering among strangers." He said those words with increasing agitation; his eyes rested on her eagerly with a wild look in them. She made a resolute effort to speak to him coldly—she called him "Mr. Linley"—she bade him good-bye.

It was useless. He stood between her and the door ; he disregarded what she had

said as if he had not heard it. " Hardly a
day passes," he owned to her, " that I don't
think of you."

" You shouldn't tell me that!"

" How can I see you again—and not tell
you?"

She burst out with a last entreaty. "For
God's sake, let us say good-bye!"

His manner became undisguisedly tender;
his language changed in the one way of all
others that was most perilous to her—he
appealed to her pity: " Oh, Sydney, it's so
hard to part with you!"

" Spare me!" she cried passionately.
" You don't know how I suffer."

" My sweet angel, I do know it—by what
I suffer myself! Do you ever feel for me
as I feel for you ?"

" Oh, Herbert! Herbert!"

" Have you ever thought of me since we
parted ?"

She had striven against herself, and against him, till her last effort at resistance was exhausted. In reckless despair she let the truth escape her at last.

"When do I ever think of anything else! I am a wretch unworthy of all the kindness that has been shown to me. I don't deserve your interest ; I don't even deserve your pity. Send me away—be hard on me—be brutal to me. Have some mercy on a miserable creature whose life is one long hopeless effort to forget you!" Her voice, her look, maddened him. He drew her to his bosom ; he held her in his arms ; she struggled vainly to get away from him. "Oh," she murmured, "how cruel you are! Remember, my dear one, remember how young I am, how weak I am. Oh, Herbert, I'm dying—dying—dying!" Her voice grew fainter and fainter ; her head sank on his breast. He lifted her face to him with whispered words of love. He kissed her again and again.

The curtains over the library entrance moved noiselessly when they were parted. The footsteps of Catherine Linley were inaudible as she passed through, and entered the room.

She stood still for a moment in silent horror.

Not a sound warned them when she advanced. After hesitating for a moment, she raised her hand towards her husband, as if to tell him of her presence by a touch ; drew it back, suddenly recoiling from her own first intention ; and touched Sydney instead.

Then, and then only, they knew what had happened.

Face to face, those three persons—with every tie that had once united them

snapped asunder in an instant—looked at
each other. The man owed a duty to the
lost creature whose weakness had appealed
to his mercy in vain. The man broke the
silence.

" Catherine——"

With immeasurable contempt looking
brightly out of her steady eyes, his wife
stopped him.

" Not a word !"

He refused to be silent. " It is I," he
said ; " I only who am to blame."

" Spare yourself the trouble of making
excuses," she answered ; " they are needless.
Herbert Linley, the woman who was once
your wife despises you."

Her eyes turned from him, and rested on
Sydney Westerfield.

" I have a last word to say to *you*. Look
at me, if you can. Listen to me, if you can."

Sydney lifted her head. She looked

vacantly at the outraged woman before her,
as if she saw a woman in a dream.

With the same terrible self-possession
which she had preserved from the first—
standing between her husband and her
governess—Mrs. Linley spoke.

"Miss Westerfield, you have saved my
child's life." She paused—her eyes still
resting on the girl's face. Deadly pale, she
pointed to her husband, and said to
Sydney : "Take him !"

She passed out of the room—and left
them together.

CHAPTER XXII.

RETROSPECT.

THE autumn holiday-time had come to an end ; and the tourists had left Scotland to the Scots.

In the dull season, a solitary traveller from the North arrived at the nearest post town to Mount Morven. A sketch-book and a colour-box formed part of his luggage, and declared him to be an artist. Falling into talk over his dinner with the waiter at the hotel, he made inquiries about a picturesque house in the neighbourhood, which showed that Mount Morven was well-known to him by reputation. When

he proposed paying a visit to the old border
fortress the next day, the waiter said:
" You can't see the house." When the
traveller asked Why, this man of few words
merely added : " Shut up."

The landlord made his appearance with a
bottle of wine, and proved to be a more
communicative person in his relations with
strangers.   Presented in an abridged form,
and in the English language, these (as he
related them) were the circumstances under
which Mount Morven had been closed to
the public.

A complete dispersion of the family had
taken place not long since.   For miles
round everybody was sorry for it.   Rich
and poor alike felt the same sympathy with
the good lady of the house.   She had been
most shamefully treated by her husband,
and by a good-for-nothing girl employed as
governess.   To put it plainly, the two had

run away together ; one report said they
had gone abroad, and another declared that
they were living in London. Mr. Linley's
conduct was perfectly incomprehensible.
He had always borne the highest character
—a good landlord, a kind father, a devoted
husband. And yet, after more than eight
years of exemplary married life, he had
disgraced himself. The minister of the
parish, preaching on the subject, had attributed this extraordinary outbreak of vice,
on the part of an otherwise virtuous man,
to a possession of the devil. Assuming
" the devil," in this case, to be only a
discreet and clerical way of alluding from
the pulpit to a woman, the landlord was
inclined to agree with the minister. After
what had happened, it was, of course, impossible that Mrs. Linley could remain in her
husband's house. She and her little girl,
and her mother, were supposed to be living

in retirement. They kept the place of their retreat a secret from everybody but Mrs. Linley's legal adviser, who was instructed to forward letters. But one other member of the family remained to be accounted for. This was Mr. Linley's younger brother; known at present to be travelling on the Continent. Two trustworthy old servants had been left in charge at Mount Morven—and there was the whole story; and that was why the house was shut up.

CHAPTER XXIII.

SEPARATION.

In a cottage on the banks of one of the Cumberland Lakes, two ladies were seated at the breakfast-table. The window of the room opened on a garden which extended to the water's edge, and on a boat-house and wooden pier beyond. On the pier a little girl was fishing, under the care of her maid. After a prevalence of rainy weather, the sun was warm this morning for the time of year ; and the broad sheet of water alternately darkened and brightened as the moving masses of cloud now gathered and now parted over the blue beauty of the sky.

The ladies had finished their breakfast; the elder of the two—that is to say Mrs. Presty—took up her knitting, and eyed her silent daughter with an expression of impatient surprise.

"Another bad night, Catherine?"

The personal attractions that distinguished Mrs. Linley were not derived from the short-lived beauty which depends on youth and health. Pale as she was, her face preserved its fine outline; her features had not lost their grace and symmetry of form. Presenting the appearance of a woman who had suffered acutely, she would have been more than ever (in the eyes of some men) a woman to be admired and loved.

"I seldom sleep well, now," she answered patiently.

"You don't give yourself a chance," Mrs. Presty remonstrated. "Here's a fine morning—come out for a sail on the lake. To-morrow there's a concert in the town— let's take tickets. There's a want of what I call elastic power in your mind, Catherine —the very quality for which your father was so remarkable ; the very quality which Mr. Presty used to say made him envy Mr. Norman. Look at your dress! Where's the common-sense, at your age, of wearing nothing but black? Nobody's dead who belongs to us, and yet you do your best to look as if you were in mourning."

" I have no heart, Mamma, to wear colours."

Mrs. Presty considered this reply to be unworthy of notice. She went on with her knitting, and only laid it down when the servant brought in the letters which had arrived by the morning's post. They were but two in number—and both were for Mrs. Linley. In the absence of any correspondence of her own, Mrs. Presty took possession of her daughter's letters.

"One addressed in the lawyer's handwriting," she announced ; "and one from Randal. Which shall I open for you first?"

"Randal's letter, if you please."

Mrs. Presty handed it across the table. "Any news is a relief from the dulness of this place," she said. "If there are no secrets, Catherine, read it out."

There were no secrets on the first page.

Randal announced his arrival in London from the Continent, and his intention of staying there for a while. He had met with a friend (formerly an officer holding high rank in the Navy) whom he was glad to see again—a rich man who used his wealth admirably in the interest of his poor and helpless fellow-creatures. A "Home," established on a new plan, was just now ing all his attention : he was devoting himself so unremittingly to the founding of this institution that his doctor predicted injury to his health at no distant date. If it was possible to persuade him to take a holiday, Randal might return to the Continent as the travelling-companion of his friend.

" This must be the man whom he first met at the club," Mrs. Presty remarked. " Well, Catherine, I suppose there is some more of it. What's the matter? Bad news?"

" Something that I wish Randal had not written. Read it yourself—and don't talk of it afterwards."

Mrs. Presty read:

" I know nothing whatever of my unfortunate brother. If you think this a too-indulgent way of alluding to a man who has so shamefully wronged you, let my conviction that he is already beginning to suffer the penalty of his crime plead my excuse. Herbert's nature is, in some respects, better known to me than it is to you. I am persuaded that your hold on his respect and his devotion is shaken— not lost. He has been misled by one of those passing fancies, disastrous and even criminal in their results, to which men are liable when they are led by no better influence than the influence of their senses. It is not, and never will be, in the nature of women to understand this. I fear I may offend you in what I am now writing ; but I must speak what I believe to be the truth, at any sacrifice. Bitter repentance (if he is not already feeling it) is in store for Herbert, when he finds himself tied to a pesron who cannot bear comparison with you. I say this, pitying the poor girl most sincerely, when I think of her youth and

her wretched past life. How it will end I
cannot presume to say. I can only acknowledge that I do not look to the future with
the absolute despair which you naturally
felt when I last saw you."

Mrs. Presty laid the letter down, privately
resolving to write to Randal, and tell him
to keep his convictions for the future to
himself. A glance at her daughter's face
warned her, if she said anything, to choose
a new subject.

The second letter still remained unnoticed. " Shall we see what the lawyer
says?" she suggested — and opened the
envelope. The lawyer had nothing to say.
He simply enclosed a letter received at his
office.

Mrs. Presty had long passed the age at
which emotion expresses itself outwardly
by a change of colour. She turned pale,

24—2

nevertheless, when she looked at the second letter.

The address was in Herbert Linley's handwriting.

CHAPTER XXIV.

WHEN she was not eating her meals or asleep in her bed, absolute silence on Mrs. Presty's part was a circumstance without precedent in the experience of her daughter. Mrs. Presty was absolutely silent now. Mrs. Linley looked up.

She at once perceived the change in her mother's face, and asked what it meant. "Mamma, you look as if something had frightened you. Is it anything in that letter?" She bent over the table, and looked a little closer at the letter. Mrs. Presty had turned it so that the address was underneath;

and the closed envelope was visible still intact. "Why don't you open it?" Mrs. Linley asked.

Mrs. Presty made a strange reply. " I am thinking of throwing it into the fire."

" My letter?"

" Yes; your letter."

" Let me look at it first."

" You had better not look at it, Catherine."

Naturally enough, Mrs. Linley remonstrated. " Surely I ought to read a letter forwarded by my lawyer. Why are you hiding the address from me? Is it from some person whose handwriting we both know?" She looked again at her silent mother—reflected—and guessed the truth. " Give it to me directly," she said; " my husband has written to me."

Mrs. Presty's heavy eyebrows gathered into a frown. " Is it possible," she asked sternly, "that you are still fond enough of that man to care about what he writes to you?" Mrs. Linley held out her hand for the letter. Her wise mother found it desirable to try persuasion next. " If you really won't give way, my dear, humour me for once. Will you let me read it to you?"

" Yes—if you promise to read every word of it."

Mrs. Presty promised (with a mental reservation), and opened the letter.

At the two first words, she stopped and began to clean her spectacles. Had her own eyes deceived her? Or had Herbert Linley actually addressed her daughter — after having been guilty of the cruellest wrong that a husband can inflict on a wife—as " Dear Catherine"? Yes : there were the words, when she put her spectacles on again. Was he in his right senses? or had he written in a state of intoxication?

Mrs. Linley waited, with a preoccupied mind: she showed no signs of impatience or surprise. As it presently appeared, she was not thinking of the letter addressed to her by Herbert, but of the letter written by Randal. "I want to look at it again." With that brief explanation she turned at once to the closing lines which had offended her when she first read them.

Mrs. Presty hazarded a guess at what was going on in her daughter's mind. "Now your husband has written to you," she said, " are you beginning to think that Randal's opinion may be worth considering again?" With her eyes still on Randal's letter, Mrs. Linley merely answered: " Why don't you begin?" Mrs. Presty began as follows, leaving out the familiarity of her son-in-law's address to his wife.

" I hope and trust you will forgive me for venturing to write to you, in consideration of the subject of my letter. I have something to say concerning our child. Although I have deserved the worst you can think of me, I believe you will not deny that even your love for our little Kitty (while we were living together) was not a truer love than mine. Bad as I am, my heart has that tender place left in it still. I cannot endure separation from my child."

Mrs. Linley rose to her feet. The first vague anticipations of future atonement and reconciliation, suggested by her brother-in-law, no longer existed in her mind: she foresaw but too plainly what was to come. " Read faster," she said, " or let me read it for myself."

Mrs. Presty went on: " There is no wish, on my part, to pain you by any needless allusion to my claims as a father. My one desire is to enter into an arrangement which shall be as just towards you, as it is towards me. I propose that Kitty shall live with her father one half of the year, and shall return to her mother's care for the other half. If there is any valid objection to this, I confess I fail to see it."

Mrs. Linley could remain silent no longer.

"Does he see no difference," she broke out, "between his position and mine? What consolation—in God's name, what consolation is left to me for the rest of my life but my child? And he threatens to separate us for six months in every year! And he takes credit to himself for an act of exalted justice on his part! Is there no such feeling as shame in the hearts of men?"

Under ordinary circumstances, her mother would have tried to calm her. But Mrs. Presty had turned to the next page of the letter, at the moment when her daughter spoke.

What she found written, on that other side, produced a startling effect on her. She crumpled the letter up in her hand, and threw it into the fireplace. It fell under the grate, instead of into the grate. With amazing activity for a woman of her age, she ran across the room to burn it. Younger and quicker, Mrs. Linley got to the fireplace first, and seized the letter. "There is something more!" she exclaimed. "And you are afraid of my knowing what it is."

"Don't read it!" Mrs. Presty called out.

There was but one sentence left to read: "If your maternal anxiety suggests any misgiving, let me add that a woman's loving care will watch over our little girl while she is under my roof. You will remember how fond Miss Westerfield was of Kitty, and you will believe me when I tell you that she is as truly devoted to the child as ever."

"I tried to prevent you from reading it," said Mrs. Presty.

Mrs. Linley looked at her mother with a strange unnatural smile.

"I wouldn't have missed this for anything!" she said. "The cruellest of all separations is proposed to me—and I am expected to submit to it, because my husband's mistress is fond of my child!" She threw the letter from her with a frantic gesture of contempt, and burst into a fit of hysterical laughter.

The old mother's instinct—not the old mother's reason—told her what to do. She drew her daughter to the open window, and called to Kitty to come in. The child (still amusing herself by fishing in the lake) laid down her rod. Mrs. Linley saw her running lightly along the little pier, on her way to the house. *That* influence effected what no other influence could have achieved.

The outraged wife controlled herself, for the sake of her child. Mrs. Presty led her out to meet Kitty in the garden; waited until she saw them together; and returned to the breakfast-room.

Herbert Linley's letter lay on the floor; his discreet mother-in-law picked it up. It could do no more harm now, and there might be reasons for keeping the husband's proposal. "Unless I am very much mistaken," Mrs. Presty concluded, "we shall hear more from the lawyer before long." She locked up the letter, and wondered what her daughter would do next.

In half an hour Mrs. Linley returned—pale, silent, self-contained.

She seated herself at her desk ; wrote literally one line; signed it without an instant's hesitation, and folded the paper. Before it was secured in the envelope, Mrs. Presty interfered with a characteristic request. "You are writing to Mr. Linley, of course," she said. "May I see it?"

Mrs. Linley handed the letter to her. The one line of writing contained these words: "I refuse positively to part with my child.—Catherine Linley."

"Have you considered what is likely to happen, when he gets this?" Mrs. Presty inquired.

"No, Mamma."

"Will you consult Randal?"

"I would rather not consult him."

"Will you let me consult him for you?"

"Thank you—no."

"Why not?"

"After what Randal has written to me, I don't attach any value to his opinion." With that reply she sent her letter to the post, and went back again to Kitty.

After this, Mrs. Presty resolved to wait the arrival of Herbert Linley's answer, and to let events take their course. The view from the window (as she passed it, walking up and down the room) offered her little help in forecasting the future. Kitty had returned to her fishing; and Kitty's mother was walking slowly up and down the pier, deep in thought. Was she thinking of what might happen, and summoning the resolution which so seldom showed itself on ordinary occasions?

CHAPTER XXV.

CONSULTATION.

No second letter arrived. But a telegram was received from the lawyer towards the end of the week.

" Expect me to-morrow on business which requires personal consultation."

That was the message. In taking the long journey to Cumberland, Mrs. Linley's legal adviser sacrificed two days of his precious time in London. Something serious must assuredly have happened.

In the meantime, who was the lawyer?

He was Mr. Sarrazin, of Lincoln's-Inn Fields.

Was he an Englishman or a Frenchman? He was a curious mixture of both. His ancestors had been among the persecuted French people who found a refuge in England, when the priest-ridden tyrant, Louis the Fourteenth, revoked the Edict of Nantes. A British subject by birth, and a thoroughly competent and trustworthy man, Mr. Sarrazin laboured under one inveterate delusion; he firmly believed that his original French nature had been completely eradicated, under the influence of our insular climate and our insular customs. No matter how often the strain of the lively French blood might assert itself, at inconvenient times and under regrettable circumstances, he never recognised this foreign side of his character. His excellent spirits, his quick sympathies, his bright mutability of mind—all those qualities, in short, which were most mischievously ready to raise distrust

in the minds of English clients, before their
sentiments changed for the better under the
light of later experience—were attributed
by Mr. Sarrazin to the exhilarating influence
of his happy domestic circumstances and his
successful professional career. His essentially English wife; his essentially English
children ; his whiskers, his politics, his um-
brella, his pew at church, his plum-pudding,
his *Times* newspaper, all answered for him
(he was accustomed to say) as an inbred
member of the glorious nation that rejoices
in hunting the fox, and believes in innumer-
able pills.

This excellent man arrived at the cottage,
desperately fatigued after his long journey,
but in perfect possession of his incomparable
temper, nevertheless.

He afforded a proof of this happy state of
mind, on sitting down to his supper. An
epicure, if ever there was one yet, he found

the solid part of the refreshments offered to
him to consist of a chop. The old French
blood curdled at the sight of it—but the
true - born Englishman heroically devoted
himself to the national meal. At the same
time the French vivacity discovered a
kindred soul in Kitty; Mr. Sarrazin became
her intimate friend in five minutes. He
listened to her and talked to her, as if
the child had been his client, and fishing
from the pier the business which had
brought him from London. To Mrs.
Presty's disgust, he turned up a corner
of the table-cloth, when he had finished his
chop, and began to conjure so deftly with
the spoons and forks that poor little Kitty
(often dull, now, under the changed
domestic circumstances of her life) clapped
her hands with pleasure, and became the
joyous child of the happy old times once
more. Mrs. Linley, flattered in her mater-

25—2

nal love and her maternal pride, never thought of recalling this extraordinary lawyer to the business that was waiting to be discussed. But Mrs. Presty looked at the clock, and discovered that her grandchild ought to have been in bed half-an-hour ago.

"Time to say good-night," the grandmother suggested.

The grandchild failed to see the subject of bed in the same light. "Oh, not yet," she pleaded; "I want to speak to Mr.——" Having only heard the visitor's name once, and not finding her memory in good working order after the conjuring, Kitty hesitated. "Isn't your name something like Saracen?" she asked.

"Very like!" cried the genial lawyer. "Try my other name, my dear. I'm Samuel as well as Sarrazin."

"Ah, that'll do," said Kitty. "Grandmamma, before I go to bed, I've something to ask Samuel."

Grandmamma persisted in deferring the question until the next morning. Samuel administered consolation before he said good-night. " I'll get up early," he whispered, " and we'll go on the pier before breakfast and fish."

Kitty expressed her gratitude in her own outspoken way. " Oh, dear, how nice it would be, Samuel, if you lived with us!" Mrs. Linley laughed for the first time, poor soul, since the catastrophe which had broken up her home. Mrs. Presty set a proper example. She moved her chair so that she faced the lawyer, and said : " Now, Mr. Sarrazin!"

He acknowledged that he understood what this meant, by a very unprofessional choice of words. " We are in a mess," he began, " and the sooner we are out of it the better."

" Only let me keep Kitty," Mrs. Linley declared, " and I'll do whatever you think right."

" Stick to that, dear Madam, when you have heard what I have to tell you—and I shall not have taken my journey in vain. In the first place, may I look at the letter which I had the honour of forwarding some days since?"

Mrs. Presty gave him Herbert Linley's letter. He read it with the closest attention, and tapped the breast-pocket of his coat when he had done.

" If I didn't know what I have got here," he remarked, " I should have said : Another person dictated this letter, and the name of the person is Miss Westerfield."

" Just my idea!" Mrs. Presty exclaimed. " There can't be a doubt of it."

" Oh, but there is very great doubt of it, Ma'am; and you will say so too when you know what your severe son-in-law threatens to do." He turned to Mrs. Linley. "After having seen that pretty little friend of mine who has just gone to bed (how much nicer it would be for all of us if we could go to bed too!) I think I know how you answered your husband's letter. But I ought perhaps to see how you have expressed yourself. Have you got a copy?"

" It was too short, Mr. Sarrazin, to make a copy necessary."

" Do you mean you can remember it?"

" I can repeat it word for word. This was my reply: I refuse, positively, to part with my child."

" No more than that?"

" No more."

Mr. Sarrazin looked at his client with un-disguised admiration. " The only time in all my long experience," he said, " in which

I have found a lady's letter capable of expressing itself strongly in few words. What a lawyer you will make, Mrs. Linley, when the rights of women invade my profession!"

He put his hand into his pocket, and produced a letter addressed to himself.

Watching him anxiously, the ladies saw his bright face become overclouded with anxiety. "I am the wretched bearer of bad news," he resumed, " and if I fidget in my chair, that is the reason for it. Let us get to the point—and let us get off it again as soon as possible. Here is a letter, written to me by Mr. Linley's lawyer. If you will take my advice you will let me say what the substance of it is, and then put it back in my pocket. I doubt if a woman has influenced these cruel instructions, Mrs. Presty; and, therefore, I doubt if a woman influenced the letter

which has led the way to them. Did I not
say just now that I was coming to the point?
and here I am wandering farther and farther
away from it. A lawyer is human; there is
the only excuse. Now, Mrs. Linley, in two
words! Your husband is determined to
have little Miss Kitty; and the law, when
he applies to it, is his obedient humble
servant."

"Do you mean that the law takes my
child away from me?"

"I am ashamed, Madam, to think that
I live by the law; but that, I must own,
is exactly what it is capable of doing in the
present case. Compose yourself, I beg and
pray. A time will come when women will
remind men that the mother bears the child
and feeds the child, and will insist that the
mother's right is the best right of the two.
In the meanwhile——"

" In the meanwhile, Mr. Sarrazin, I won't submit to the law."

" Quite right, Catherine!" cried Mrs. Presty. " Exactly what I should do, in your place."

Mr. Sarrazin listened patiently. " I am all attention, good ladies," he said with the gentlest resignation. " Let me hear how you mean to do it."

The good ladies looked at each other. They discovered that it is one thing to set an abuse at defiance in words, and another thing to apply the remedy in deeds. The kind-hearted lawyer helped them with a suggestion. " Perhaps you think of making your escape with the child, and taking refuge abroad?"

Mrs. Linley eagerly accepted the hint. " The first train to-morrow morning starts at half-past seven," she said. " We might

catch some foreign steamer that sails from
the east coast of Scotland."

Mrs. Presty, keeping a wary eye on
Mr. Sarrazin, was not quite so ready as her
daughter in rushing at conclusions. " I am
afraid," she acknowledged, " our worthy
friend sees some objection. What is it?"

"I don't presume to offer a positive
opinion, Ma'am; but I think Mr. Linley
and his lawyer have their suspicions.
Plainly speaking, I am afraid spies are set
to watch us already."

" Impossible !"

" You shall hear. I travel second-class ;
one saves money, and one finds people to
talk to—and at what sacrifice? Only a
hard cushion to sit on! In the same carriage with me there was a very conversible
person—a smart young man with flaming
red hair. When we took the omnibus at
your station here, all the passengers got

out in the town except two. I was one
exception, and the smart young man was
the other. When I stopped at your gate,
the omnibus went on a few yards, and set
down my fellow-traveller at the village inn.
My profession makes me sly. I waited a
little before I rang your bell; and, when I
could do it without being seen, I crossed
the road, and had a look at the inn. There
is a moon to-night; I was very careful.
The young man didn't see me. But I saw
a head of flaming hair, and a pair of amiable
blue eyes, over the blind of a window; and
it happened to be that one window of the
inn which commands a full view of your
gate. Mere suspicion, you will say! I
can't deny it, and yet I have my reasons
for suspecting. Before I left London, one
of my clerks followed me in a great hurry
to the terminus, and caught me as I was
opening the carriage door. 'We have just

made a discovery,' he said; 'you and Mrs. Linley are to be reckoned up.' Reckoned up is, if you please, detective English for being watched. My clerk might have repeated a false report, of course. And my fellow-traveller might have come all the way from London to look out of the window of an inn, in a Cumberland village. What do you think yourselves?"

It seemed to be easier to dispute the law than to dispute Mr. Sarrazin's conclusions.

"Suppose I choose to travel abroad, and to take my child with me," Mrs. Linley persisted, "who has any right to prevent me?"

Mr. Sarrazin reluctantly reminded her that the father had a right. "No person—not even the mother—can take the child out of the father's custody," he said, "except with the father's consent. His authority is the supreme authority—unless it

happens that the law has deprived him
of his privilege, and has expressly confided
the child to the mother's care. Ha!" cried
Mr. Sarrazin, twisting round in his chair,
and fixing his keen eyes on Mrs. Presty,
"look at your good mother; *she* sees what
I am coming to."

"I see something more than you think,"
Mrs. Presty answered. "If I know anything of my daughter's nature, you will
find yourself, before long, on delicate
ground."

"What do you mean, Mamma?"

Mrs. Presty had lived in the past age
when persons occasionally used metaphor
as an aid to the expression of their ideas.
Being called upon to explain herself, she
did it in metaphor, to her own entire satis-
faction.

"Our learned friend here reminds me,
my dear Catherine, of a traveller exploring

a strange town. He takes a turning, in the confident expectation that it will reward him by leading to some satisfactory result —and he finds himself in a blind alley, or, as the French put it (I speak French fluently), in a *cool de sack.* Do I make my meaning clear, Mr. Sarrazin?"

"Not the least in the world, Ma'am."

"How very extraordinary! Perhaps I have been misled by my own vivid imagination. Let me endeavour to express myself plainly—let me say that my fancy looks prophetically at what you are going to do, and sincerely wishes you well out of it. Pray go on."

"And pray speak more plainly than my mother has spoken," Mrs. Linley added. "As I understand what you said just now, there is a law, after all, that will protect me in the possession of my little girl. I don't care what it costs ; I want that law."

" May I ask first," Mr. Sarrazin stipu-
lated, " whether you are positively resolved
not to give way to your husband in this
matter of Kitty?"

" Positively."

" One more question, if you please, on a
matter of fact.   I have heard that you were
married in Scotland.   Is that true?"

" Quite true."

Mr. Sarrazin exhibited himself once more
in a highly unprofessional aspect.   He
clapped his hands, and cried " Bravo!" as
if he had been in a theatre.

Mrs. Linley caught the infection of the
lawyer's excitement.   " How dull I am!"
she exclaimed.   " There is a thing they
call 'incompatibility of temper'—and married people sign a paper at the lawyer's,
and promise never to trouble each other
again as long as they both live.   And
they're readier to do it in Scotland than

they are in England. That's what you
mean—isn't it?"

Mr. Sarrazin found it necessary to re-
assume his professional character.

" No, indeed, Madam," he said, " I should
be unworthy of your confidence if I proposed nothing better than that. You can
only secure the sole possession of little
Kitty by getting the help of a Judge——"

" Get it at once," Mrs. Linley interposed.

" And you can only prevail on the Judge
to listen to you," Mr. Sarrazin proceeded,
" in one way. Summon your courage,
Madam. Apply for a Divorce."

There was a sudden silence. Mrs. Linley
rose trembling, as if she saw—not good
Mr. Sarrazin—but the devil himself tempt-
ing her. " Do you hear that ?" she said to
her mother.

Mrs. Presty only bowed.

" Think of the dreadful exposure !"

Mrs. Presty bowed again.

The lawyer had his opportunity now. " Well, Mrs. Linley," he asked, " what do you say ?"

" No—never !" She made that positive reply ; and disposed beforehand of everything that might have been urged, in the way of remonstrance and persuasion, by leaving the room. The two persons who remained, sitting opposite to each other, took opposite views.

" Mr. Sarrazin, she won't do it."

" Mrs. Presty, she will."

CHAPTER XXVI.

DECISION.

PUNCTUAL to his fishing appointment with Kitty, Mr. Sarrazin was out in the early morning, waiting on the pier.

Not a breath of wind was stirring; the lazy mist lay asleep on the farther shore of the lake. Here and there only, the dim tops of the hills rose like shadows cast by the earth on the faint grey of the sky. Nearer at hand, the waters of the lake showed a gloomy surface; no birds flew over the colourless calm; no passing insects tempted the fish to rise. From time to time a last-left leaf on the wooded shore

26—2

dropped noiselessly and died. No vehicles passed as yet on the lonely road; no voices were audible from the village; slow and straight, wreaths of smoke stole their way out of the chimneys, and lost their vapour in the misty sky. The one sound that disturbed the sullen repose of the morning was the tramp of the lawyer's footsteps, as he paced up and down the pier. He thought of London and its ceaseless traffic, its roaring high-tide of life in action—and he said to himself, with the strong conviction of a town-bred man: How miserable this is!

A voice from the garden cheered him, just as he reached the end of the pier for the fiftieth time, and looked with fifty-fold intensity of dislike at the dreary lake.

There stood Kitty behind the garden-gate, with a fishing-rod in each hand. A tin box was strapped on one side of her

little body, and a basket on the other.
Burdened with these impediments, she required assistance. Susan had let her out
of the house; and Samuel must now open
the gate for her. She was pleased to
observe that the raw morning had reddened
her friend's nose; and she presented her
own nose to notice as exhibiting perfect
sympathy in this respect. Feeling a misplaced confidence in Mr. Sarrazin's knowledge and experience as an angler, she
handed the fishing-rods to him. "My
fingers are cold," she said; "you bait the
hooks." He looked at his young friend
in silent perplexity; she pointed to the tin
box. "Plenty of bait there, Samuel; we
find maggots do best." Mr. Sarrazin eyed
the box with undisguised disgust; and
Kitty made an unexpected discovery.
"You seem to know nothing about it,"
she said. And Samuel answered cordially,

" Nothing!"   In five minutes more he
found himself by the side of his young
friend—with his hook baited, his line in
the water, and strict injunctions to keep an
eye on the float.

They began *to* fish.

Kitty looked at her ompanion, and
looked away again in silence. By way of
encouraging her to talk, the good-natured
lawyer alluded to what she had said when
they parted overnight. " You wanted to
ask me something," he reminded her.
" What is it?"

Without one preliminary word of warning to prepare him for the shock, Kitty
answered : " I want you to tell me what
has become of Papa, and why Syd has gone
away and left me. You know who Syd is,
don't you?"

The only alternative left to Mr. Sarrazin
was to plead ignorance. While Kitty

was instructing him on the subject of her governess, he had time to consider what he should say to her next. The result added one more to the lost opportunities of Mr. Sarrazin's life.

"You see," the child gravely continued, "you are a clever man; and you have come here to help Mamma. I have got that much out of Grandmamma, if I have got nothing else. Don't look at me; look at your float. My Papa has gone away, and Syd has left me without even saying good-bye, and we have given up our nice old house in Scotland and come to live here. I tell you I don't understand it. If you see your float begin to tremble, and then give a little dip down as if it was going to sink, pull your line out of the water; you will most likely find a fish at the end of it. When I ask Mamma what all this means, she says there is a reason, and I am not old

enough to understand it, and she looks unhappy, and she gives me a kiss, and it ends
in that way. You've got a bite: no you
haven't; it's only a nibble; fish are so sly.
And Grandmamma is worse still. Sometimes she tells me I'm a spoilt child; and
sometimes she says well-behaved little girls
don't ask questions. That's nonsense—
and I think it's hard on me. You look
uncomfortable. Is it my fault? I don't
want to bother you; I only want to know
why Syd has gone away. When I was
younger I might have thought the fairies
had taken her. Oh, no! that won't do any
longer; I'm too old. Now tell me."

Mr. Sarrazin weakly attempted to gain
time: he looked at his watch. Kitty
looked over his shoulder: " Oh, we needn't
be in a hurry; breakfast won't be ready for
half an hour yet. Plenty of time to talk of
Syd; go on."

Most unwisely (seeing that he had to deal with a clever child, and that child a girl), Mr. Sarrazin tried flat denial as a way out of the difficulty. He said : " I don't know why she has gone away." The next question followed instantly : " Well, then, what do you *think* about it ?" In sheer despair, the persecuted friend said the first thing that came into his head.

" I think she has gone to be married."

Kitty was indignant. " Gone to be married, and not tell me !" she exclaimed. " What do you mean by that ?"

Mr. Sarrazin's professional experience of women and marriages failed to supply him with an answer. In this difficulty he exerted his imagination, and invented something that no woman ever did yet. " She's waiting," he said, " to see how her marriage succeeds, before she tells anybody about it."

This sounded probable to the mind of a child. " I hope she hasn't married a beast," Kitty said, with a serious face and an ominous shake of the head. " When shall I hear from Syd?"

Mr. Sarrazin tried another prevarication— with better results this time. " You will be the first person she writes to, of course." As that excusable lie passed his lips, his float began to tremble. Here was a chance of changing the subject—" I've got a fish !" he cried.

Kitty was immediately interested. She threw down her own rod, and assisted her ignorant companion. A wretched little fish appeared in the air, wriggling. " It's a roach," Kitty pronounced. " It's in pain," the merciful lawyer added ; " give it to me." Kitty took it off the hook, and obeyed. Mr. Sarrazin with humane gentleness of handling put it back into the water.

" Go, and God bless you," said this excellent man, as the roach disappeared
joyously with a flick of its tail. Kitty was
scandalised. " That's not sport!" she said.
" Oh, yes, it is," he answered—" sport to
the fish."

They went on with their angling. What
embarrassing question would Kitty ask
next ? Would she want to be told why
her father had left her? No : the last
image in the child's mind had been the
image of Sydney Westerfield. She was still
thinking of it when she spoke again.

· " I wonder whether you're right about
Syd ?" she began. " You might be mistaken,
mightn't you? I sometimes fancy Mamma
and Sydney may have had a quarrel. Would
you mind asking Mamma if that's true ?"
the affectionate little creature said anxiously.
" You see, I can't help talking of Syd, I'm
so fond of her ; and I do miss her so dread-

fully every now and then; and I'm afraid
—oh, dear, dear, I'm afraid I shall never
see her again!" She let her rod drop on
the pier, and put her little hands over her
face, and burst out crying.

Shocked and distressed, good Mr. Sarrazin
kissed her, and consoled her, and told
another excusable lie. "Try to be com-
forted, Kitty; I'm sure you will see her again."

His conscience reproached him as he held
out that false hope. It could never be!
The one unpardonable sin, in the judgment
of fallible human creatures like herself, was
the sin that Sydney Westerfield had committed. Is there something wrong in
human nature? or something wrong in
human laws? All that is best and noblest
in us feels the influence of love—and the
rules of society declare that an accident of
position shall decide whether love is a virtue
or a crime.

These thoughts were in the lawyer's mind. They troubled and disheartened him : it was a relief rather than an interruption when he felt Kitty's hand on his arm. She had dried her tears, with a child's happy facility in passing from one emotion to another, and was now astonished and interested by a marked change in the weather.

"Look for the lake!" she cried. "You can't see it."

A dense white fog was closing round them. It's stealthy advance over the water had already begun to hide the boat-house at the end of the pier from view. The raw cold of the atmosphere made the child shiver. As Mr. Sarrazin took her hand to lead her indoors, he turned and looked back at the faint outline of the boat-house, disappearing in the fog. Kitty wondered. "Do you see anything?" she asked.

He answered that there was nothing to

see, in the absent tone of a man busy with his own thoughts. They took the garden path which led to the cottage. As they reached the door he roused himself, and looked round again in the direction of the invisible lake.

" Was the boat-house of any use now," he inquired—" was there a boat in it for instance ?"   " There was a capital boat, fit to go anywhere."   " And a man to manage it ?"   " To be sure ! the gardener was the man ; he had been a sailor once ; and he knew the lake as well as——" Kitty stopped, at a loss for a comparison. " As well as you know your multiplication-table?" said Mr. Sarrazin, dropping his serious questions on a sudden. Kitty shook her head. " Much better," she honestly acknowledged.

Opening the breakfast-room door they saw Mrs. Presty making coffee. Kitty at once retired. When she had been fishing, her Grandmamma inculcated habits of order by directing her to take the rods to pieces, and to put them away in their cases in the lumber room. While she was absent, Mr. Sarrazin profited by the opportunity, and asked if Mrs. Linley had thought it over in the night, and had decided on applying for a Divorce.

"I know nothing about my daughter," Mrs. Presty answered, "except that she had a bad night. Thinking, no doubt, over your advice," the old lady added with a mischievous smile.

"Will you kindly inquire if Mrs. Linley has made up her mind yet?" the lawyer ventured to say.

"Isn't that your business?" Mrs. Presty asked slily. "Suppose you write a little note, and I will send it up to her room." The worldly-wisdom which prompted this suggestion contemplated a possible necessity for calling a domestic council, assembled to consider the course of action which Mrs. Linley would do well to adopt. If the influence of her mother was among the forms of persuasion which might be tried, that wary relative manœuvred to make the lawyer speak first, and so to reserve to herself the advantage of having the last word.

Patient Mr. Sarrazin wrote the note.

He modestly asked for instructions ; and he was content to receive them in one word —Yes or No. In the event of the answer being Yes, he would ask for a few minutes' conversation with Mrs. Linley, at her earliest convenience. That was all.

The reply was returned in a form which left Yes to be inferred : " I will receive you as soon as you have finished your breakfast."

CHAPTER XXVII.

RESOLUTION.

HAVING read Mrs. Linley's answer, Mr. Sarrazin looked out of the breakfast-room window, and saw that the fog had reached the cottage. Before Mrs. Presty could make any remark on the change in the weather, he surprised her by an extraordinary question.

"Is there an upper room here, Ma'am, which has a view of the road before your front gate?"

"Certainly!"

"And can I go into it without disturbing anybody?"

Mrs. Presty said, " Of course!" with an uplifting of her eyebrows which expressed astonishment not unmixed with suspicion. " Do you want to go up now?" she added, " or will you wait till you have had your breakfast?"

" I want to go up, if you please, before the fog thickens. Oh, Mrs. Presty, I am ashamed to trouble you! Let the servant show me the room."

No. For the first time in her life, Mrs. Presty insisted on doing servant's duty. If she had been crippled in both legs, her curiosity would have helped her to get up the stairs on her hands. " There!" she said, opening the door of the upper room, and placing herself exactly in the middle of it, so that she could see all round her: " Will that do for you?"

Mr. Sarrazin went to the window; hid himself behind the curtain; and cautiously peeped out. In half a minute he turned his back on the misty view of the road, and said to himself : " Just what I expected."

Other women might have asked what this mysterious proceeding meant. Mrs. Presty's sense of her own dignity adopted a system of independent discovery. To Mr. Sarrazin's amusement, she imitated him to his face. Advancing to the window, she too hid herself behind the curtain, and she too peeped out. Still following her model, she next turned her back on the view—and then she became herself again. " Now we have both looked out of window," she said to the lawyer, in her own inimitably impudent way, " suppose we compare our impressions."

This was easily done. They had both seen the same two men, walking backwards and forwards opposite the front gate of the cottage. Before the advancing fog made it

27—2

impossible to identify him, Mr. Sarrazin had
recognised, in one of the men, his agreeable
fellow-traveller on the journey from London.
The other man—a stranger—was in all
probability an assistant spy obtained in the
neighbourhood. This discovery suggested
serious embarrassment in the future. Mrs.
Presty asked what was to be done next.
Mr. Sarrazin answered: "Let us have our
breakfast."

In another quarter of an hour they were
both in Mrs. Linley's room.

Her agitated manner, her reddened eyes,
showed that she was still suffering under
the emotions of the past night. The moment the lawyer approached her, she crossed
the room with hurried steps, and took both
his hands in her trembling grasp. "You
are a good man, you are a kind man," she
said to him wildly; "you have my truest

respect and regard. Tell me, are you really
—really—really sure that the one way in
which I can keep my child with me is the
way you mentioned last night?"

Mr. Sarrazin led her gently back to her
chair.

The sad change in her startled and distressed him. Sincerely, solemnly even, he
declared that the one alternative before her
was the alternative that he had mentioned.
He entreated her to control herself. It was
useless; she still held him as if she was
holding to her last hope.

" Listen to me!" she cried. " There's
something more; there's another chance for
me. I must, and will, know what you
think of it."

" Wait a little. Pray wait a little!"

" No! not a moment. Is there any hope
in appealing to the lawyer whom Mr. Linley
has employed? Let me go back with you

to London. I will persuade him to exert his influence—I will go down on my knees to him—I will never leave him till I have won him over to my side—I will take Kitty with me; he shall see us both, and pity us, and help us!"

"Hopeless. Quite hopeless, Mrs. Linley."

"Oh, don't say that!"

"My dear lady, my poor dear lady, I must say it. The man you are talking of is the last man in the world to be influenced as you suppose. He is notoriously a lawyer, and nothing but a lawyer. If you tried to move him to pity you, he would say, 'Madam, I am doing my duty to my client;' and he would ring his bell and have you shown out. Yes! even if he saw you crushed and crying at his feet."

Mrs. Presty interfered for the first time.

"In your place, Catherine," she said, "I would put my foot down on that man and

crush *him.* Consent to the Divorce, and
you may do it."

Mrs. Linley lay prostrate in her chair
The excitement which had sustained her
thus far seemed to have sunk with the sinking of her last hope. Pale, exhausted,
yielding to hard necessity, she looked up
when her mother said, "Consent to the
Divorce," and answered, "I have consented."

"And trust me," Mr. Sarrazin said fer-
vently, "to see that justice is done, and to
protect you in the meanwhile."

Mrs. Presty added her tribute of consolation.

"After all," she asked, "what is there to
terrify you in the prospect of a Divorce?
You won't hear what people say about it—
for we see no society now. And, as for the
newspapers, keep them out of the house."

Mrs. Linley answered with a momentary
revival of energy.

"It is not the fear of exposure that has tortured me," she said. "When I was left in the solitude of the night, my heart turned to Kitty; I felt that any sacrifice of myself might be endured for her sake. It's the remembrance of my marriage, Mr. Sarrazin, that is the terrible trial to me. Those whom God has joined together, let no man put asunder. Is there nothing to terrify me in setting that solemn command at defiance? I do it—oh, I do it—in consenting to the Divorce! I renounce the vows which I bound myself to respect in the presence of God; I profane the remembrance of eight happy years, hallowed by true love. Ah, you needn't remind me of what my husband has done. I don't forget how cruelly he has wronged me; I don't forget that his own act has cast me from him. But whose act destroys our marriage? Mine! mine! Forgive me, Mamma; forgive me, my kind friend—the horror that I have of myself forces its way to my lips. No more of it! My child is my one treasure left. What must I do next? What must I sign? What must I sacrifice? Tell me—and it shall be done. I submit! I submit!"

Delicately and mercifully Mr. Sarrazin answered that sad appeal.

All that his knowledge, experience, and resolution could suggest, he addressed to Mrs. Presty. Mrs. Linley could listen or not listen, as her own wishes inclined. In the one case or in the other, her interests would be equally well served. The good lawyer kissed her hand. "Rest, and recover," he whispered. And then he turned to her mother — and became a man of business once more.

"The first thing I shall do, Ma'am, is to telegraph to my agent in Edinburgh. He will arrange for the speediest possible hearing of our case in the Court of Session. Make your mind easy so far."

Mrs. Presty's mind was by this time equally inaccessible to information and advice. "I want to know what is to be done with those two men who are watching the gate," was all she said in the way of reply.

Mrs. Linley raised her head in alarm.

"Two!" she exclaimed—and looked at Mr. Sarrazin. "You only spoke of one last night."

"And I add another this morning. Rest your poor head, Mrs. Linley; I know how it aches; I know how it burns." He still persisted in speaking to Mrs. Presty. "One of those two men will follow me to the station, and see me off on my way to London. The other will look after you, or your daughter, or the maid, or any other person who may try to get away into hiding with Kitty. And they are both keeping close to the gate, in the fear of losing sight of us in the fog."

"I wish we lived in the Middle Ages!" said Mrs. Presty.

"What would be the use of that, Ma'am?"

"Good heavens, Mr. Sarrazin, don't you see? In those grand old days you would have taken a dagger, and the gardener would have taken a dagger, and you would have stolen out, and stabbed those two villains as a matter of course. And this is the age of progress! The vilest rogue in existence is a sacred person whose life we are bound to respect. Ah, what good that national hero would have done who put his barrels of gunpowder in the right place on the Fifth of November! I have always said it, and I stick to it, Guy Fawkes was a great states-man."

In the meanwhile Mrs. Linley was not

resting, and not listening to the expression of her mother's political sentiments. She was intently watching Mr. Sarrazin's face.

"There is danger threatening us," she said. "Do you see a way out of it?"

To persist in trying to spare her was plainly useless. Mr. Sarrazin answered her directly.

"The danger of legal proceedings to obtain possession of the child," he said, "is more near and more serious than I thought it right to acknowledge, while you were in doubt which way to decide. I was careful —too careful, perhaps—not to unduly influence you in a matter of the utmost importance to your future life. But you have made up your mind. I don't scruple now to remind you that an interval of time must pass before the decree for your Divorce can be pronounced, and the care of the child be legally secured to the mother. The only doubt and the only danger are there. If you are not frightened by the prospect of a desperate venture which some women would shrink from, I believe I see a way of baffling the spies."

Mrs. Linley started to her feet. " Say what I am to do," she cried, " and judge for yourself if I am as easily frightened as some women."

The lawyer pointed with a persuasive smile to her empty chair. " If you allow yourself to be excited," he said, " you will frighten *me*. Please—oh, please sit down again !"

Mrs. Linley felt the strong will, asserting itself in terms of courteous entreaty. She obeyed. Mrs. Presty had never admired the lawyer as she admired him now. " Is that how you manage your wife?" she asked.

Mr. Sarrazin was equal to the occasion,

whatever it might be. "In your time, Ma'am," he said, "did you reveal the mysteries of conjugal life?" He turned to Mrs. Linley. "I have something to ask first," he resumed, "and then you shall hear what I propose. How many people serve you in this cottage?"

"Three. Our landlady, who is house-keeper and cook. Our own maid. And the landlady's daughter, who does the housework."

"Any out-of-door servants?"

"Only the gardener."

"Can you trust these people?"

"In what way, Mr. Sarrazin?"

"Can you trust them with a secret which only concerns yourself?"

"Certainly! The maid has been with us for years; no truer woman ever lived. The good old landlady often drinks tea with us. Her daughter is going to be married; and I have given the wedding dress. As for the gardener, let Kitty settle the matter with him, and I answer for the rest. Why are you pointing to the window?"

" Look out, and tell me what you see."

" I see the fog."

" And I, Mrs. Linley, have seen the boathouse. While the spies are watching your gate, what do you say to crossing the lake, under cover of the fog?"

FOURTH BOOK.

CHAPTER XXVIII.

MR. RANDAL LINLEY.

Winter had come and gone; spring was nearing its end, and London still suffered under the rigid regularity of easterly winds. Although in less than a week summer would begin with the first of June, Mr. Sarrazin was glad to find his office warmed by a fire, when he arrived to open the letters of the day.

The correspondence in general related exclusively to proceedings connected with the law. Two letters only presented an exception to the general rule. The first

28—2

was addressed in Mrs. Linley's handwriting, and bore the postmark of Hanover. Kitty's mother had not only succeeded in getting to the safe side of the lake—she and her child had crossed the German Ocean as well. In one respect her letter was a remarkable composition. Although it was written by a lady, it was short enough to be read in less than a minute :

" MY DEAR MR. SARRAZIN,

"I have just time to write by this evening's post. Our excellent courier has satisfied himself that the danger of discovery has passed away. The wretches have been so completely deceived that they are already on their way back to England, to lie in wait for us at Folkestone and Dover. To-morrow morning we leave this charming place—oh, how unwillingly!— for Bremen, to catch the steamer to Hull.

Y~~ou~~ shall hear from me again on our arrival. G~~ratefu~~lly yours,

"CATHERINE LINLEY."

Mr. Sarrazin put this letter into a private drawer, and smiled as he turned the key. " Has she made up her mind at last?" he asked himself. " But for the courier, I shouldn't feel sure of her, even now!"

The second letter agreeably surprised him. It announced that the writer had just returned from the United States; it invited him to dinner that evening; and it was signed " Randal Linley." In Mr. Sarrazin's estimation, Randal had always occupied a higher place than his brother. The lawyer had known Mrs. Linley before her marriage, and had been inclined to think that she would have done wisely if she had given her hand to the younger brother instead of the elder. His acquaintance

with Randal ripened rapidly into friend-
ship. But his relations with Herbert
made no advance towards intimacy: there
was a gentlemanlike cordiality between
them, and nothing more.

At seven o'clock the two friends sat at a
snug little table, in the private room of an
hotel, with an infinite number of questions
to ask of each other, and with nothing
to interrupt them but a dinner of such
extraordinary merit that it insisted on
being noticed, from the first course to the
last.

Randal began. " Before we talk of
anything else," he said, " tell me about
Catherine and the child. Where are they?'

" On their way to England, after a resi-
dence in Germany."

" And the old lady?"

" Mrs. Presty has been staying with
friends in London."

"What! have they parted company? Has there been a quarrel?"

"Nothing of the sort; a friendly separation, in the strictest sense of the word. Oh, Randal, what are you about? Don't put pepper into this perfect soup. It's as good as the *gras double* at the Café Anglais in Paris."

"So it is; I wasn't paying the proper attention to it. But I am anxious about Catherine. Why did she go abroad?'

"Haven't you heard from her?"

"Not for six months or more. I innocently vexed her by writing a little too hopefully about Herbert. Mrs. Presty answered my letter, and recommended me not to write again. It isn't like Catherine to bear malice."

' Don't even think such a thing possible!" the lawyer answered earnestly. "Attribute her silence to the right cause. Terrible anxieties have been weighing on her mind since you went to America."

" Anxieties caused by my brother? Oh, I hope not!"

" Caused entirely by your brother—if I must tell the truth. Can't you guess how?"

" Is it the child? You don't mean to tell me that Herbert has taken Kitty away from her mother!"

" While I am her mother's lawyer, my friend, your brother won't do that. Welcome back to England in the first glass of sherry; good wine, but a little too dry for my taste. No, we won't talk of domestic troubles just yet. You shall hear all about it after dinner. What made you go to America? You haven't been delivering lectures, have you?"

" I have been enjoying myself among the most hospitable people in the world."

Mr. Sarrazin shook his head ; he had a

case of copyright in hand just then. "A people to be pitied," he said.

"Why?"

"Because their Government forgets what is due to the honour of the nation."

"How?"

"In this way. The honour of a nation which confers right of property in works of art, produced by its own citizens, is surely concerned in protecting from theft works of art produced by other citizens."

"That's not the fault of the people."

"Certainly not. I have already said it's the fault of the Government. Let's attend to the fish now."

Randal took his friend's advice. "Good sauce, isn't it?" he said.

The epicure entered a protest. "Good?" he repeated. "My dear fellow, it's absolute perfection. I don't like to cast a slur on English cookery. But think of melted butter, and tell me if anybody but a foreigner (I don't like foreigners, but I give them their due) could have produced this white wine sauce? So you really had no particular motive in going to America?"

"On the contrary, I had a very particular motive. Just remember what my life used to be when I was in Scotland—and look at my life now! No Mount Morven; no model farm to look after; no pleasant Highland neighbours; I can't go to my brother while he is leading his present life; I have hurt Catherine's feelings; I have lost dear little Kitty; I am not obliged to earn my living (more's the pity); I don't care about politics; I have a pleasure in eating harmless creatures, but no pleasure in shooting them. What is there left for me to do, but to try change of scene, and go roaming about the world, a restless creature without an object in life? Have I done something

wrong again ? It isn't the pepper this
time—and yet you're looking at me as if I
was trying your temper."

. The French side of Mr. Sarrazin's nature
had got the better of him once more. He
pointed indignantly to a supreme prepara-
tion of fowl on his friend's plate. "Do
I actually see you picking out your truffles,
and putting them on one side?" he asked.

"Well," Randal acknowledged, "I don't
care about truffles."

Mr. Sarrazin rose, with his plate in his
hand and his fork ready for action. He
walked round the table to his friend's side,
and reverently transferred the neglected
truffles to his own plate. "Randal, you
will live to repent this," he said solemnly.
"In the meantime, I am the gainer." Until
he had finished the truffles, no word fell
from his lips. "I think I should have
enjoyed them more," he remarked, "if I

had concentrated my attention by closing
my eyes; but you would have thought
I was going to sleep." He recovered his
English nationality, after this, until the
dessert had been placed on the table, and
the waiter was ready to leave the room. At
that   auspicious   moment, he   underwent
another relapse. He insisted on sending
his compliments and thanks to the cook.

"At last," said Randal, "we are by
ourselves—and now I want to know why
Catherine went to Germany."

CHAPTER XXIX.

MR. SARRAZIN.

As a lawyer, Randal's guest understood that a narrative of events can only produce the right effect, on one condition: it must begin at the beginning. Having related all that had been said and done during his visit to the cottage, including his first efforts in the character of an angler under Kitty's supervision, he stopped to fill his glass again —and then astonished Randal by describing the plan that he had devised for escaping from the spies by crossing the lake in the fog.

" What did the ladies say to it?" Randal inquired. " Who spoke first?"

"Mrs. Presty, of course! She objected to risk her life on the water, in a fog. Mrs. Linley showed a resolution for which I was not prepared. She thought of Kitty, saw the value of my suggestion, and went away at once to consult with the landlady. In the meantime I sent for the gardener, and told him what I was thinking of. He was one of those stolid Englishmen, who possess resources which don't express themselves outwardly. Judging by his face, you would have said he was subsiding into slumber under the infliction of a sermon, instead of listening to a lawyer proposing a stratagem. When I had done, the man showed the metal he was made of. In plain English, he put three questions which gave me the highest opinion of his intelligence. ' How much luggage, sir?' ' As little as they can conveniently take with them,' I said. 'How many persons?' 'The two ladies, the child, and myself.' 'Can you row, sir?' 'In any water you like, Mr. gardener, fresh or salt.' Think of asking Me, an athletic Englishman, if I could row! In an hour more we were ready to embark, and the blessed fog was thicker than ever. Mrs. Presty yielded under protest; Kitty was wild with delight; her mother was quiet and resigned. But one circumstance occurred that I didn't quite understand—the presence of a stranger on the pier with a gun in his hand."

"You don't mean one of the spies?"

"Nothing of the sort; I mean an idea of the gardener's. He had been a sailor in his time—and that's a trade which teaches a man (if he's good for anything) to think, and act on his thought, at one and the same moment. He had taken a peep at the blackguards in front of the house, and had recognised the shortest of the two as a native of the place, perfectly well aware that one of the features attached to the cottage was a boathouse. 'That chap is not such a fool as he looks,' says the gardener. 'If he mentions the boathouse, the other fellow from London may have his suspicions. I thought I would post my son on the pier— that quiet young man there with the gun— to keep a look-out. If he sees another boat (there are half-a-dozen on this side of the lake) putting off after us, he has orders to fire, on the chance of our hearing him. A little notion of mine, sir, to prevent our being surprised in the fog. Do you see any objection to it?' Objection! In the days when diplomacy was something more than a solemn pretence, what a member of Congress that gardener would have made! Well, we shipped our oars, and away we went. Not quite haphazard—for we had a compass with us. Our course was as straight as we could go, to a village on the opposite side of the lake, called Brightfold. Nothing happened for the first quarter of an hour—and then, by the living Jingo (excuse my vulgarity), we heard the gun!"

"What did you do?"

"Went on rowing, and held a council. This time I came out as the clever one of the party. The men were following us in the dark; they would have to guess at the direction we had taken, and they would most likely assume (in such weather as we had) that we should choose the shortest way across the lake. At my suggestion we changed our course, and made for a large town, higher up on the shore, called Tawley. We landed, and waited for events, and made no discovery of another boat behind us. The fools had justified my confidence in them—they had gone to Brightfold. There was half-an-hour to spare before the next train came to Tawley; and the fog was beginning to lift on that side of the lake. We looked at the shops; and I made a purchase in the town."

"Stop a minute," said Randal. "Is Brightfold on the railway?"

"No."

"Is there an electric telegraph at the place?"

"Yes."

"That was awkward, wasn't it? The first thing those men would do would be to telegraph to Tawley."

"Not a doubt of it. How would they describe us, do you think?"

Randal answered. "A middle-aged gentleman—two ladies, one of them elderly —and a little girl. Quite enough to identify

you at Tawley, if the station-master understood the message."

"Shall I tell you what the station-master
discovered, with the message in his hand ?
No elderly lady, no middle-aged gentleman ;
nothing more remarkable than *one* lady—
and a little boy."

Randal's face brightened. "You parted
company, of course," he said ; "and you
disguised Kitty ! How did you manage
it ?"

"Didn't I say just now that we looked at
the shops, and that I made a purchase in
the town ? A boy's ready-made suit—not
at all a bad fit for Kitty! Mrs. Linley put
on the suit, and tucked up the child's hair
under a straw hat, in an empty yard—no
idlers about in that bad weather. We said
good-bye, and parted, with grievous mis-
givings on my side, which proved (thank
God!) to have been quite needless. Kitty

and her mother went to the station, and
Mrs. Presty and I hired a carriage, and
drove away to the head of the lake, to catch
the train to London. Do you know,
Randal, I have altered my opinion of Mrs.
Presty."

Randal smiled. " You too have found
something in that old woman," he said,
" which doesn't appear on the surface."

" The occasion seems to bring that something out," the lawyer remarked. " When
I proposed the separation, and mentioned
my reasons, I expected to find some
difficulty in persuading Mrs. Presty to give
up the adventurous journey with her
daughter and her grandchild. I reminded
her that she had friends in London who
would receive her, and got snubbed for
taking the liberty. ' I know that as well
as you do. Come along—I'm ready to go
with you.' It isn't agreeable to my self-

esteem to own it, but I expected to hear
her say that she would consent to any
sacrifice for the sake of her dear daughter.
No such clap-trap as that passed her lips.
She owned the true motive with a superiority
to cant which won my sincerest respect.
'I'll do anything,' she said, 'to baffle
Herbert Linley and the spies he has set to
watch us.' I can't tell you how glad I was
that she had her reward on the same day.
We were too late at the station, and we had
to wait for the next train. And what do
you think happened ? The two scoundrels
followed *us* instead of following Mrs.
Linley! They had inquired no doubt at
the livery stables where we hired the
carriage—had recognised the description of
us—and had taken the long journey to
London for nothing. Mrs. Presty and I
shook hands at the terminus the best friends
that ever travelled together, with the best

of motives. After that, I think I deserve another glass of wine."

"Go on with your story, and you shall have another bottle!" cried Randal. "What did Catherine and the child do after they left you?"

"They did the safest thing—they left England. Mrs. Linley distinguished herself on this occasion. It was her excellent idea to avoid popular ports of departure, like Folkestone and Dover, which were sure to be watched, and to get away (if the thing could be done) from some place on the east coast. We consulted our guide and found that a line of steamers sailed from Hull to Bremen once a week. A tedious journey from our part of Cumberland, with some troublesome changing of trains, but they got there in time to embark. My first news of them reached me in a telegram from Bremen. There they waited for further

instructions. I sent the instructions by a
thoroughly capable and trustworthy man—
an Italian courier, known to me by an
experience of twenty years. Shall I confess
it ? I thought I had done rather a clever
thing in providing Mrs. Linley with a friend
in need while I was away from her."

"I think so too," said Randal.

"Wrong, completely wrong. I had made
a mistake—I had been too clever, and I got
my reward accordingly. You know how I
advised Mrs. Linley ?"

"Yes. You persuaded her, with the
greatest difficulty, to apply for a Divorce."

"Very well. I had made all the necessary
arrangements for the trial, when I received
a letter from Germany. My charming client
had changed her mind, and declined to
apply for the Divorce. There was my reward
for having been too clever !"

"I don't understand you."

"My dear fellow, you are dull to-night. I had been so successful in protecting Mrs. Linley and the child, and my excellent courier had found such a charming place of retreat for them in one of the suburbs of Hanover, that 'she saw no reason now for taking the shocking course that I had recommended to her—so repugnant to all her most cherished convictions; so sinful and so shameful in its doing of evil that good might come. Experience had convinced her that (thanks to me) there was no fear of Kitty being discovered and taken from her. She therefore begged me to write to my agent in Edinburgh, and tell him that her application to the court was withdrawn.' Ah, you understand my position at last. The headstrong woman was running a risk which renewed all my anxieties. By every day's post I expected to hear that she had paid the penalty of her folly, and that your brother had succeeded in getting possession of the child. Wait a little before you laugh at me. But for the courier, the thing would have really happened a week since."

Randal looked astonished. "Months must have passed," he objected. "Surely, after that lapse of time, Mrs. Linley must have been safe from discovery."

"Take your own positive view of it! I only know that the thing happened. And why not? The luck had begun by being on our side—why shouldn't the other side have had its turn next?"

"Do you really believe in luck?"

"Devoutly. A lawyer must believe in something. He knows the law too well to put any faith in that; and his clients present to him (if he is a man of any feeling) a hideous view of human nature. The poor devil believes in luck—rather than believe in nothing. I think it quite likely that accident helped the person employed by the husband to discover the wife and child. Anyhow, Mrs. Linley and Kitty were seen in the streets of Hanover; seen, recognised, and followed. The courier happened to be with them—luck again! For thirty years and more, he had been travelling in every part of Europe; there was not a landlord of the smallest pretensions anywhere who didn't know him and like him. 'I pretended not to see that anybody was following us,' he said (writing from Hanover to relieve my anxiety); 'and I took the ladies to an hotel. The hotel possessed two merits from our point of view—it had a way out at the back, through the stables, and it was kept by a landlord who was an excellent good friend of mine. I arranged with him what he was to say when inquiries were made; and I kept my poor ladies prisoners in their lodging for three days. The end of it is that Mr. Linley's policeman has gone away to watch the Channel steam-service, while we return quietly by way of Bremen and Hull.' There is the courier's account of it. I have only to add that poor Mrs. Linley has been fairly frightened into sub-mission. She changes her mind again, and pledges herself once more to apply for the Divorce. If we are only lucky enough to get our case heard without any very serious delay, I am not afraid of my client slipping through my fingers for the second time. When will the courts of session be open to us? You have lived in Scotland, Randal ——"

" But I haven't lived in the courts of law. I wish I could give you the information you want."

Mr. Sarrazin looked at his watch. " For all I know to the contrary," he said, " we may be wasting precious time while we are talking here. Will you excuse me if I go away to my club?"

"Are you going in search of information?"

"Yes. We have some inveterate old whist players who are always to be found in the card-room. One of them formerly practised, I believe, in the Scotch courts. It has just occurred to me that the chance is worth trying."

"Will you let me know if you succeed?" Randal asked.

The lawyer took his hand at parting. "You seem to be almost as anxious about it as I am," he said.

"To tell you the truth, I am a little alarmed when I think of Catherine. If there is another long delay, how do we know what may happen before the law has confirmed the mother's claim to the child? Let me send one of the servants here to

wait at your club. Will you give him a
line telling me when the trial is likely to
take place?"

"With the greatest pleasure. Good-
night."

Left alone, Randal sat by the fireside for
awhile, thinking of the future. The prospect,
as he saw it, disheartened him. As a means
of employing his mind on a more agreeable
subject for reflection, he opened his travelling desk, and took out two or three letters.
They had been addressed to him, while he
was in America, by Captain Bennydeck.

The captain had committed an error of
which most of us have been guilty in our
time. He had been too exclusively devoted
to work that interested him, to remember
what was due to the care of his health.
The doctor's warnings had been neglected;
his over-strained nerves had given way; and
the man whose strong constitution had re-

sisted cold and starvation in the Arctic wastes, had broken down under stress of brain work in London.

This was the news which the first of the letters contained.

The second, written under dictation, alluded briefly to the remedies suggested. In the captain's case, the fresh air recommended was the air of the sea. At the same time he was forbidden to receive either letters or telegrams, during his absence from town, until the doctor had seen him again. These instructions pointed, in Captain Bennydeck's estimation, to sailing for pleasure's sake, and therefore to hiring a yacht.

The third, and last, letter announced that the yacht had been found, and described the captain's plans when the vessel was ready for sea.

He proposed to sail here and there about

the Channel, wherever it might please the
wind to take him. Friends would accompany him, but not in any number.
The yacht was not large enough to accommodate comfortably more than one or two
guests at a time. Every now and then, the
vessel would come to an anchor in the bay
of the little coast town of Sandyseal, to
accommodate friends going and coming,
and (in spite of medical advice) to receive
letters. " You may have heard of Sandyseal," the Captain wrote, " as one of the
places which have lately been found out by
the doctors. They are recommending the
air to patients suffering from nervous dis-
orders, all over England. The one hotel in
the place, and the few cottages which let
lodgings, are crammed as I hear; and the
speculative builder is beginning his opera-
tions at such a rate, that Sandyseal will be
no longer recognisable in a few months

more. Before the crescents and terraces
and grand hotels turn the town into a
fashionable watering-place, I want to take a
last look at scenes familiar to me under
their old aspect. If you are inclined to
wonder at my feeling such a wish as this,
I can easily explain myself. Two miles
inland from Sandyseal, there is a lonely old
moated house. In that house I was born.
When you return from America, write to
me at the post-office, or at the hotel (I am
equally well-known in both places), and let
us arrange for a speedy meeting. I wish I
could ask you to come and see me in my
birthplace. It was sold, years since, under
instructions in my father's will, and was
purchased for the use of a community of
nuns. We may look at the outside, and
we can do no more. In the meantime,
don't despair of my recovery; the sea is my
old friend, and my trust is in God's mercy."

These last lines were added in a postscript:

" Have you heard any more of that poor girl, the daughter of my old friend Roderick Westerfield—whose sad story would never have been known to me but for you? I feel sure that you have good reasons for not telling me the name of the man who has misled her, or the address at which she may be found. But you may one day be at liberty to break your silence. In that case, don't hesitate to do so because there may happen to be obstacles in my way. No difficulties discourage me, when my end in view is the saving of a soul in peril."

Randal returned to his desk to write to the Captain. He had only got as far as the first sentences, when the servant returned with the lawyer's promised message. Mr. Sarrazin's news was communicated in these cheering terms:—

"I am a firmer believer in luck than ever. If we only make haste—and won't I make haste!—we may get the Divorce, as I calculate, in three weeks' time."

CHAPTER XXX.

THE LORD PRESIDENT.

Mrs. Linley's application for a Divorce was heard in the first division of the Court of Session at Edinburgh, the Lord President being the Judge.

To the disappointment of the large audience assembled, no defence was attempted on the part of the husband—a wise decision, seeing that the evidence of the wife and her witnesses was beyond dispute. But one exciting incident occurred towards the close of the proceedings. Sudden illness made Mrs. Linley's removal necessary, at the moment of all others most interesting to herself—the moment before the Judge's decision was announced.

But, as the event proved, the poor lady's withdrawal was the most fortunate circumstance that could have occurred, in her own interests. After condemning the husband's conduct with unsparing severity, the Lord President surprised most of the persons present by speaking of the wife in these terms :

Grievously as Mrs. Linley has been injured, the evidence shows that she was herself by no means free from blame. She has been guilty, to say the least of it, of acts of indiscretion. When the criminal attachment which had grown up between Mr. Herbert Linley and Miss Westerfield had been confessed to her, she appears to have most unreasonably overrated whatever merit there might have been in their resistance to the final temptation. She

was indeed so impulsively ready to forgive (without waiting to see if the event
justified the exercise of mercy) that she
owns to having given her hand to Miss
Westerfield, at parting, not half an hour
after that young person's shameless forget-
fulness of the claims of modesty, duty, and
gratitude had been first communicated to
her.   To say that this was the act of an in-
considerate woman, culpably indiscreet, and
I had almost added, culpably indelicate, is
only to say what she has deserved.   On
the next occasion to which I feel bound to
advert, her conduct was even more deserv-
ing of censure.   She herself appears to have
placed the temptation under which he fell
in her husband's way, and so (in some
degree at least) to have provoked the catastrophe which has brought her before this
court.   I allude, it is needless to say, to
her having invited the governess—then out

of harm's way; then employed elsewhere—
to return to her house, and to risk (what
actually occurred) a meeting with Mr.
Herbert Linley when no third person
happened to be present. I know that
the maternal motive which animated Mrs.
Linley is considered, by many persons, to
excuse and even to justify that most regrettable act; and I have myself allowed
(I fear weakly allowed) more than due
weight to this consideration in pronouncing
for the Divorce. Let me express the
earnest hope that Mrs. Linley will take
warning by what has happened ; and, if
she finds herself hereafter placed in other
circumstances of difficulty, let me advise
her to exercise more control over impulses
which one might expect perhaps to find in
a young girl, but which are neither natural
nor excusable in a woman of her age."

His lordship then decreed the Divorce in

the customary form; giving the custody of
the child to the mother.

*   ·   *   *   *   *

As fast as a hired carriage could take
him, Mr. Sarrazin drove from the court to
Mrs. Linley's lodgings, to tell her that the
one great object of securing her right to
her child had been achieved.

At the door he was met by Mrs. Presty.
She was accompanied by a stranger, whose
medical services had been required. Interested professionally in hearing the result of
the trial, this gentleman volunteered to
communicate the good news to his patient.
He had been waiting to administer a composing draught, until the suspense from
which Mrs. Linley was suffering might be
relieved, and a reasonable hope be entertained that the medicine would produce the
right effect. With that explanation he left
the room.

While the doctor was speaking, Mrs. Presty was drawing her own conclusions from a close scrutiny of Mr. Sarrazin's face.

"I am going to make a disagreeable remark," she announced. " You look ten years older, sir, than you did when you left us this morning to go to the Court. Do me a favour—come to the sideboard." The lawyer having obeyed, she poured out a glass of wine. " There is the remedy," she resumed, " when something has happened to worry you."

" 'Worry' isn't the right word," Mr. Sarrazin declared. " I'm furious! It's a most improper thing for a person in my position to say of a person in the Lord President's position; but I do say it—he ought to be ashamed of himself."

"After giving us our Divorce!" Mrs. Presty exclaimed. " What has he done?" .

Mr. Sarrazin repeated what the Judge had said of Mrs. Linley. " In my opinion," he added, " such language as that is an insult to your daughter."

" And yet," Mrs. Presty repeated, " he has given us our Divorce." She returned to the sideboard, poured out a second dose of the remedy against worry, and took it herself. " What sort of character does the Lord President bear?" she asked when she had emptied her glass.

This seemed to be an extraordinary question to put, under the circumstances. Mr. Sarrazin answered it, however, to the best of his ability. " An excellent character," he said—" that's the unaccountable part of it. I hear that he is one of the most careful and considerate men who ever sat on the bench. Excuse me, Mrs. Presty, I didn't intend to produce that impression on you."

" What impression, Mr. Sarrazin?"

" You look as if you thought there was some excuse for the Judge."

" That's exactly what I do think."

" You find an excuse for him?"

" I do."

" What is it, Ma'am?"

" Constitutional infirmity, sir."

" May I ask of what nature?"

" You may.   Gout."

Mr. Sarrazin thought he understood her at last.   " You know the Lord President," he said.

Mrs. Presty denied it positively.   " No, Mr. Sarrazin, I don't get at it in that way. I merely consult my experience of another official person of high rank, and apply it to the Lord President.   You know that my first husband was a Cabinet Minister?"

" I have heard you say so, Mrs. Presty, on more than one occasion."

" Very well.   You may also have heard
that the late Mr. Norman was a remarkably
well-bred man.   In and out of the House
of Commons, courteous almost to a fault.
One day I happened to interrupt him when
he was absorbed over an Act of Parliament.
Before I could apologise—I tell you this in
the strictest confidence—he threw the Act
of Parliament at my head.   Ninety-nine
women out of a hundred would have
thrown it back again.   Knowing his constitution, I decided on waiting a day or
two.   On the second day, my anticipations
were realised.   Mr. Norman's great toe
was as big as my fist, and as red as a
lobster ; he apologised for the Act of Parliament with tears in his eyes.   Suppressed
gout in Mr. Norman's temper ; suppressed
gout in the Lord President's temper.   *He*
will have a toe; and, if I can prevail upon
my daughter to call upon him, I have not

the least doubt he will apologise to her with tears in *his* eyes."

This interesting experiment was never destined to be tried. Right or wrong, Mrs. Presty's theory remained the only explanation of the Judge's severity. Mr. Sarrazin attempted to change the subject. Mrs. Presty had not quite done with it yet. " There is one more thing I want to say," she proceeded. " Will his lordship's remarks appear in the newspapers?"

"Not a doubt of it."

" In that case I will take care (for my daughter's sake) that no newspapers enter the house to-morrow. As for visitors, we needn't be afraid of them. Catherine is not likely to be able to leave her room; the worry of this miserable business has quite broken her down."

The doctor returned at that moment.

Without taking the old lady's gloomy

view of his patient, he admitted that she was in a low nervous condition; and he had reason to suppose, judging by her reply to a question which he had ventured to put, that she had associations with Scotland which made a visit to that country far from agreeable to her. His advice was that she should leave Edinburgh as soon as possible, and go South. If the change of climate led to no improvement, she would at least be in a position to consult the best physicians in London. In a day or two more it would be safe to remove her—provided she was not permitted to exhaust her strength by taking long railway journeys.

Having given his advice, the doctor took leave. Soon after he had gone, Kitty made her appearance, charged with a message from Mrs. Linley's room.

" Hasn't the physic sent your mother to sleep yet?" Mrs. Presty inquired.

Kitty shook her head. "Mamma wants to go away to-morrow, and no physic will make her sleep till she has seen you, and settled about it. That's what she told me to say. If *I* behaved in that way about my physic, I should catch it."

Mrs. Presty left the room ; watched by her granddaughter with an appearance of anxiety which it was not easy to understand.

"What's the matter?" Mr. Sarrazin asked. "You look very serious to-day."

Kitty held up a warning hand. "Grandmamma sometimes listens at doors," she whispered; "I don't want her to hear me." She waited a little longer, and then approached Mr. Sarrazin, frowning mysteriously. "Take me up on your knee," she said. "There's something wrong going on in this house."

Mr. Sarrazin took her on his knee, and

rashly asked what had gone wrong. Kitty's reply puzzled him.

"I go to Mamma's room every morning when I wake," the child began. "I get into her bed, and I give her a kiss, and I say 'Good morning'—and sometimes, if she isn't in a hurry to get up, I stop in her bed, and go to sleep again. Mamma thought I was asleep this morning. I wasn't asleep —I was only quiet. I don't know why I was quiet."

Mr. Sarrazin's kindness still encouraged her. "Well," he said, "and what happened after that?"

"Grandmamma came in. She told Mamma to keep up her spirits. She says, 'It will be all over in a few hours more.' She says, 'What a burden it will be off your mind.' She says, 'Is that child asleep?' And Mamma says, 'Yes.' And Grandmamma took one of Mamma's towels.

And I thought she was going to wash herself. What would *you* have thought?"

Mr. Sarrazin began to doubt whether he would do well to discuss Mrs. Presty's object in taking the towel. He only said "Go on."

" Grandmamma dipped it into the water-jug," Kitty continued with a grave face; " but she didn't wash herself. She went to one of Mamma's boxes. Though she's so old, she's awfully strong, I can tell you. She rubbed off the luggage-label in no time. Mamma says, ' What are you doing that for?' And Grandmamma says—this is the dreadful thing that I want you to explain; oh, I can remember it all; it's like learning lessons, only much nicer—Grandmamma says, ' Before the day's over, the name on your boxes will be your name no longer.'"

Mr. Sarrazin now became aware of the labyrinth into which his young friend had innocently led him. The Divorce, and the wife's inevitable return (when the husband was no longer the husband) to her maiden name—these were the subjects on which Kitty's desire for enlightenment applied to the wisest person within her reach, her mother's legal adviser.

Mr. Sarrazin tried to put her off his knee. She held him round the neck. He thought of the railway as a promising excuse, and told her he must go back to London. She held him a little tighter. " I really can't wait, my dear;" he got up as he said it. Kitty hung on to him with her legs as well as her arms, and finding the position uncomfortable, lost her temper. " Mamma's going to have a new name," she shouted, as if the lawyer had suddenly become deaf. " Grandmamma says she must be Mrs. Norman. And I must be Miss Norman. I won't ! Where s Papa ?

I want to write to him ; I know he won't allow it. Do you hear? Where's Papa?"

She fastened her little hands on Mr. Sarrazin's coat collar and tried to shake him, in a fury of resolution to know what it all meant. At that critical moment Mrs. Presty opened the door, and stood petrified on the threshold.

" Hanging on to Mr. Sarrazin with her arms *and* her legs !" exclaimed the old lady. " You little wretch, which are you, a monkey or a child?"

The lawyer gently deposited Kitty on the floor.

" Mind this, Samuel," she whispered, as he set her down on her feet, " I won't be Miss Norman."

Mrs. Presty pointed sternly to the open door. " You were screaming just now, when quiet in the house is of the utmost importance to your mother. If I hear you again, bread and water and no doll for the rest of the week."

Kitty retired in disgrace, and Mrs. Presty sharpened her tongue on Mr. Sarrazin next. " I'm astonished, sir, at your allowing that impudent grandchild of mine to take such liberties with you. Who would suppose that you were a married man, with children of your own?"

" That's just the reason, my dear madam," Mr. Sarrazin smartly replied. "I romp with my own children — why not with Kitty? Can I do anything for you in London?" he went on, getting a little nearer to the door ; " I leave Edinburgh by the next train. And I promise you," he added, with the spirit of mischief twinkling in his eyes, " this shall be my last confidential interview with your grandchild. When she wants to ask any more questions, I transfer her to you."

Mrs. Presty looked after the retreating lawyer thoroughly mystified. What " confidential interview "? What " questions "? After some consideration, her experience of her granddaughter suggested that a little exercise of mercy might be attended with the right result. She looked at a cake on the sideboard. " I have only to forgive Kitty," she decided, " and the child will talk about it of her own accord."

CHAPTER XXXI.

OF the friends and neighbours who had associated with Herbert Linley, in bygone days, not more than two or three kept up their intimacy with him at the later time of his disgrace. Those few, it is needless to say, were men.

One of the faithful companions, who had not shrunk from him yet, had just left the London hotel at which Linley had taken rooms for Sydney Westerfield and himself— in the name of Mr. and Mrs. Herbert. This old friend had been shocked by the change for the worse which he perceived in the fugitive master of Mount Morven. Linley's stout figure of former times had fallen away, as if he had suffered under long illness ; his healthy colour had faded ; he made an effort to assume the hearty manner that had once been natural to him, which was simply pitiable to see. " After sacrificing all that makes life truly decent and truly enjoyable for a woman, he has got nothing, not even false happiness, in return !" With that dreary conclusion the retiring visitor descended the hotel steps, and went his way · along the street.

Linley returned to the newspaper which he had been reading, when his friend was shown into the room.

Line by line, he followed the progress of the law report, which informed its thousands of readers that his wife had divorced him, and had taken lawful possession of his child. Word by word, he dwelt with morbid attention on the terms of crushing severity in which the Lord President had spoken of Sydney Westerfield and of himself. Sentence by sentence, he read the reproof inflicted on the unhappy woman whom he had vowed to love and cherish. And then —even then—urged by his own self-tor-.menting suspicion, he looked for more. On the opposite page there was a leading article, presenting comments on the trial, written in a tone of lofty and virtuous regret ; taking the wife's side against the Judge, but declaring, at the same time, that no condemnation of the conduct of the husband and the governess could be too merciless, and no misery that might overtake them in the future more than they had deserved.

He threw the newspaper on the table at his side, and thought over what he had read.

If he had done nothing else, he had

drained the bitter cup to the dregs. When he looked back, he saw nothing but the life that he had wasted. When his thoughts turned to the future, they confronted a prospect empty of all promise to a man still in the prime of life. Wife and child were as completely lost to him as if they had been dead—and it was the wife's doing. Had he any right to complain? Not the shadow of a right. As the newspapers said, he had deserved it.

The clock roused him, striking the hour.

He rose hurriedly, and advanced towards the window. As he crossed the room, he passed by a mirror. His own sullen despair looked at him in the reflection of his face. "She will be back directly," he remembered; "she mustn't see me like this!" He went on to the window to divert his mind (and so to clear his face) by watching the stream of life flowing by in the busy street.

Artificial cheerfulness, assumed love in Sydney's presence—that was what his life had come to already.

If he had known that she had gone out, seeking a temporary separation, with *his* fear of self-betrayal—if he had suspected that she too had thoughts which must be concealed; sad forebodings of losing her hold on his heart, terrifying suspicions that he was already comparing her, to her own disadvantage, with the wife whom he had deserted—if he had made these discoveries, what would the end have been? But she had, thus far, escaped the danger of exciting his distrust. That she loved him, he knew. That she had begun to doubt his attachment to her he would not have believed, if his oldest friend had declared it on the best evidence. She had said to him, that morning, at breakfast : " There was a good woman who used to let lodgings here in

London, and who was very kind to me when I was a child;" and she had asked leave to go to the house, and inquire if that friendly landlady was still living—with nothing visibly constrained in her smile, and with no faltering tone in her voice. It was not until she was out in the street, that the tell-tale tears came into her eyes, and the bitter sigh broke from her, and mingled its little unheard misery with the grand rise and fall of the tumult of London life. While he was still at the window, he saw her crossing the street on her way back to him. She came into the room with her complexion heightened by exercise ; she kissed him, and said with her pretty smile : " Have you been lonely without me?" Who would have supposed that the torment of distrust, and the dread of desertion, were busy at this woman's heart?

He placed a chair for her, and seating

himself by her side, asked if she felt tired.
Every attention that she could wish for
from the man whom she loved, offered with
every appearance of sincerity on the surface!
She met him half-way, and answered as if
her mind was quite at ease.

"No, dear, I'm not tired—but I'm glad
to get back."

"Did you find your old landlady still
alive?"

"Yes. But oh, so altered, poor thing!
The struggle for life must have been a hard
one, since I last saw her."

" She didn't recognise you, of course?"

"Oh! no. She looked at me and my
dress in great surprise, and said her lodgings
were hardly fit for a young lady like me. It
was too sad. I said I had known her
lodgings well, many years ago—and, with
that to prepare her, I told her who I was.
Ah, it was a melancholy meeting for both of

us. She burst out crying when I kissed her; and I had to tell her that my mother was dead, and my brother lost to me in spite of every effort to find him. I asked to go into the kitchen, thinking the change would be a relief to both of us. The kitchen used to be a paradise to me in those old days; it was so warm to a half-starved child —and I always got something to eat when I was there. You have no idea, Herbert, how poor and how empty the place looked to me now. I was glad to get out of it, and go upstairs. There was a lumber-room at the top of the house; I used to play in it, all by myself. More changes met me the moment I opened the door."

"Changes for the better?"

"My dear, it couldn't have changed for the worse! My dirty old play-room was cleaned and repaired; the lumber taken away, and a nice little bed in one corner.

Some clerk in the city had taken the room
—I shouldn't have known it again. But
there was another surprise waiting for me ;
a happy surprise this time. In cleaning out
the garret, what do you think the landlady
found? Try to guess."

Anything to please her! Anything to
make her think that he was as fond of her
as ever! "Was it something you had left
behind you," he said, "at the time when
you lodged there?"

"Yes! you are right at the first guess—
a little memorial of my father. Only some
torn crumpled leaves from a book of
children's songs that he used to teach
me to sing; and a small packet of his
letters, which my mother may have thrown
aside and forgotten. See! I have brought
them back with me; I mean to look over
the letters at once—but this doesn't interest
you."

" Indeed it does."

He made that considerate reply mechanically, as if he was thinking of something else. She was afraid to tell him plainly that she saw this; but she could venture to say that he was not looking well. " I have noticed it for some time past," she confessed. " You have been accustomed to live in the country; I am afraid London doesn't agree with you."

He admitted that she might be right; still speaking absently, still thinking of the Divorce. She laid the packet of letters and the poor relics of the old song-book on the table, and bent over him. Tenderly, and a little timidly, she put her arm round his neck. " Let us try some purer air," she suggested; " the seaside might do you good. Don't you think so?"

"I daresay, my dear. Where shall we go?"

" Oh, I leave that to you."

" No, Sydney. It was I who proposed coming to London. You shall decide this time."

She submitted, and promised to think of it. Leaving him, with the first expression of trouble that had shown itself in her face, she took up the songs, and put them into the pocket of her dress. On the point of removing the letters next, she noticed the newspaper on the table. " Anything interesting to-day?" she asked—and drew the newspaper towards her to look at it. He took it from her suddenly, almost roughly. The next moment he apologised for his rudeness. " There is nothing worth reading in the paper," he said, after begging her pardon. " You don't care about politics, do you?"

Instead of answering, she looked at him attentively.

The heightened colour which told of

recent exercise, healthily enjoyed, faded from her face. She was silent; she was pale. A little confused, he smiled uneasily. " Surely," he resumed, trying to speak gaily, " I haven't offended you ?"

" There is something in the newspaper," she said, " which you don't want me to read."

He denied it—but he still kept the newspaper in his own possession. Her voice sank low ; her face turned paler still.

" Is it all over?" she asked. " And is it put in the newspaper?"

" What do you mean?"

" I mean the Divorce."

He went back again to the window, and looked out. It was the easiest excuse that he could devise for keeping his face turned away from her. She followed him.

" I don't want to read it, Herbert. I only ask you to tell me if you are a free man again."

Quiet ‑ as it was, her tone left him no
alternative but to treat her brutally or
to reply. Still looking out at the street, he
said " Yes."

" Free to marry, if you like?" she persisted.

He said " Yes " once more—and kept his
face steadily turned away from her. She
waited awhile. He neither moved nor
spoke.

Surviving the slow death little by little
of all her other illusions, one last hope had
lingered in her heart. It was killed by that
cruel look, fixed on the view of the street.

" I'll try to think of a place that we can
go to at the seaside." Having said those
words she slowly moved away to the door,
and turned back, remembering the packet
of letters. She took it up, paused, and
looked towards the window. The street
still interested him. She left the room.

CHAPTER XXXII.

MISS WESTERFIELD.

SHE locked the door of her bedchamber, and threw off her walking dress; light as it was, she felt as if it would stifle her. Even the ribbon round her neck was more than she could endure, and breathe freely. Her over-burdened heart found no relief in tears. In the solitude of her room she thought of the future. The dreary foreboding of what it might be, filled her with a superstitious dread from which she recoiled. One of the windows was open already; she threw up the other to get more air. In the cooler atmosphere her memory recovered itself;

she recollected the newspaper that Herbert had taken from her. Instantly she rang for the maid. "Ask the first waiter you see downstairs for to-day's newspaper; anyone will do, so long as I don't wait for it." The report of the Divorce—she was in a frenzy of impatience to read what *he* had read—the report of the Divorce.

When her wish had been gratified, when she had read it from beginning to end, one vivid impression only was left on her mind. She could think of nothing but what the Judge had said, in speaking of Mrs. Linley.

A cruel reproof, and worse than cruel, a public reproof, administered to the generous friend, the true wife, the devoted mother—and for what? For having been too ready to forgive the wretch who had taken her husband from her, and had repaid a hundred acts of kindness by unpardonable ingratitude.

32—2

She fell on her knees; she tried wildly to pray for inspiration that should tell her what to do. "Oh, God, how can I give that woman back the happiness of which I have robbed her!"

The composing influence of prayer on a troubled mind was something that she had heard of. It was not something that she experienced now. An overpowering impatience to make the speediest and completest atonement possessed her. Must she wait till Herbert Linley no longer concealed that he was weary of her, and cast her off? No! It should be her own act that parted them, and that did it at once. She threw open the door, and hurried half-way down the stairs before she remembered the one terrible obstacle in her way—the Divorce.

Slowly and sadly she submitted, and went back to her room.

There was no disguising it; the two who

had once been husband and wife were parted irrevocably—by the wife's own act. Let him repent ever so sincerely, let him be ever so ready to return, would the woman whose faith Herbert Linley had betrayed, take him back? The Divorce, the merciless Divorce, answered :—No!

She paused, thinking of the marriage that was now a marriage no more. The toilet table was close to her; she looked absently at her haggard face in the glass. What a lost wretch she saw! The generous impulses which other women were free to feel were forbidden luxuries to her. She was ashamed of her wickedness; she was eager to sacrifice herself, for the good of the once-dear friend whom she had wronged. Useless longings! Too late! too late!

She regretted it bitterly. Why?

Comparing Mrs. Linley's prospects with hers, was there anything to justify regret

for the divorced wife? She had her sweet
little child to make her happy; she had a
fortune of her own to lift her above sordid
cares; she was still handsome, still a woman
to be admired. While she held her place in
the world as high as ever, what was the
prospect before Sydney Westerfield? The
miserable sinner would end as she had deserved to end. Absolutely dependent on a
man, who was at that moment perhaps
lamenting the wife whom he had deserted
and lost, how long would it be before she
found herself an outcast, without a friend to
help her—with a reputation hopelessly lost
—face to face with the temptation to drown
herself or poison herself, as other women
had drowned themselves or poisoned themselves, when the brightest future before
them was rest in death?

If she had been a few years older, Herbert
Linley might never again have seen her a

living creature. But she was too young to
follow any train of repellent thought per-
sistently to its end. The man she had
guiltily (and yet how naturally) loved was
lord and master in her heart, doubt him as
she might. Even in his absence he pleaded
with her to have some faith in him still.

She reviewed his language and his conduct towards her, when she had returned
that morning from her walk. He had been
kind and considerate; he had listened to her
little story of the relics of her father, found
in the garret, as if her interests were his
interests. There had been nothing to dis-
appoint her, nothing to complain of, until
she had rashly attempted to discover whether
he was free to make her his wife. She had
only herself to blame if he was cold and
distant when she had alluded to that delicate
subject, on the day when he first knew that
the Divorce had been granted, and his child

had been taken from him. · And yet, he might have found a kinder way of reproving a sensitive woman than looking into the street—as if he had forgotten her in the interest of watching the strangers passing by! Perhaps he was not thinking of the strangers; perhaps his mind was dwelling fondly and regretfully on his wife?

Instinctively, she felt that her thoughts were leading her back again to a state of doubt, from which her youthful hopefulness recoiled. Was there nothing she could find to do which would offer some other subject to occupy her mind than herself and her future?

Looking absently round the room, she noticed the packet of her father's letters placed on the table by her bedside.

The first three letters that she examined, after untying the packet, were briefly written, and were signed by names un-

known to her. They all related to race-
horses, and to cunningly devised bets which
were certain to make the fortunes of the
clever gamblers on the turf, who laid them.
Absolute indifference on the part of the
winners to the ruin of the losers, who were
not in the secret, was the one feeling in
common, which her father's correspondents
presented. In mercy to his memory she
threw the letters into the empty fireplace,
and destroyed them by burning.

The next letter which she picked out
from the little heap was of some length, and
was written in a clear and steady hand. By
comparison with the blotted scrawls which
she had just burnt, it looked like the letter
of a gentleman. She turned to the signa-
ture. The strange surname struck her; it
was " Bennydeck."

Not a common name, and not a name
which seemed to be altogether unknown to

her.   Had she heard her father mention it
at home in the time of her early childhood?
There were no associations with it that she
could now call to mind.

She read the letter.   It addressed her
father familiarly as " My dear Roderick,"
and it proceeded in these words:—

" The delay in the sailing of your ship
offers me an opportunity of writing to you
again.   My last letter told you of my
father's death.   I was then quite unprepared
for an event which has happened, since that
affliction befel me.   Prepare yourself to be
surprised.   Our old moated house at Sandyseal, in which we have spent so many happy
holidays when we were schoolfellows, is
sold.

" You will be almost as sorry as I was to
hear this; and you will be quite as surprised
as I was, when I tell you that Sandyseal

Place has become a Priory of English Nuns, of the order of St. Benedict.

"I think I see you look up from my letter, with your big black eyes staring straight before you, and say and swear that this must be one of my mystifications. Unfortunately (for I am fond of the old house in which I was born) it is only too true. The instructions in my father's will, under which Sandyseal has been sold, are peremptory. They are the result of a promise made, many years since, to his wife.

"You and I were both very young when my poor mother died; but I think you must remember that she, like the rest of her family, was a Roman Catholic.

"Having reminded you of this, I may next tell you that Sandyseal Place was my mother's property. It formed part of her marriage portion, and it was settled on my father if she died before him, and if she left no female child to survive her. I am her only child. My father was therefore dealing with his own property when he ordered the house to be sold. His will leaves the purchase-money to me. I would rather have kept the house.

"But why did my mother make him promise to sell the place at his death?

"A letter, attached to my father's will, answers this question, and tells a very sad story. In deference to my mother's wishes it was kept strictly a secret from me while my father lived.

"There was a younger sister of my mother's who was the beauty of the family; loved and admired by everybody who was acquainted with her. It is needless to make this long letter longer by dwelling on the girl's miserable story. You have heard it of other girls, over and over again. She loved and trusted; she was deceived and deserted. Alone and friendless in a foreign country; her fair fame blemished; her hope in the future utterly destroyed, she attempted to drown herself. This took place in France. The best of good women—a Sister of Charity—happened to be near enough to the river to rescue her. She was sheltered; she was pitied; she was encouraged to return to her family. The poor deserted creature absolutely refused; she could never forget that she had disgraced them. The good Sister of Charity won her confidence. A retreat which would hide her from the world, and devote her to religion for the rest of her days, was the one end to her wasted life that she longed for. That end was attained in a Priory of Benedictine Nuns, established in France. There she found protection and peace— there she passed the remaining years of her life among devoted Sister-friends—and there she died a quiet and even a happy death.

" You will now understand how my mother's grateful remembrance associated her with the interests of more, than one community of Nuns; and you will not need to be told what she had in mind when she obtained my father's promise at the time of her last illness.

" He at once proposed to bequeath the house as a free gift to the Benedictines. My mother thanked him and refused. She was thinking of me. 'If our son fails to inherit the house from his father,' she said, 'it is only right that he should have the value of the house in money. Let it be sold.'

" So here I am—rich already—with this additional sum of money in my banker's care.

" My idea is to invest it in the Funds, and

to let it thrive at interest, until I grow older, and retire perhaps from service in the Navy. The later years of my life may well be devoted to the founding of a charitable institution, which I myself can establish and direct. If I die first—oh, there is a chance of it! We may have a naval war, perhaps, or I may turn out one of those incorrigible madmen who risk their lives in Arctic exploration. In case of the worst, therefore, I shall leave the interests of my contemplated Home in your honest and capable hands. For the present good-bye, and a prosperous voyage outward bound."

So the letter ended.

Sydney dwelt with reluctant attention on the latter half of it. The story of the unhappy favourite of the family had its own melancholy and sinister interest for her. She felt the foreboding that it might, in

some of its circumstances, be her story too
—without the peaceful end. Into what
community of merciful women could *she* be
received, in her sorest need? What religious
consolations would encourage her penitence?
What prayers, what hopes, would reconcile
her, on her deathbed, to the common
doom?

She sighed as she folded up Captain
Bennydeck's letter, and put it in her bosom,
to be read again. "If my lot had fallen
among good people," she thought, "perhaps
I might have belonged to the Church which
took care of that poor girl."

Her mind was still pursuing its own sad
course of inquiry: she was wondering in
what part of England Sandyseal might be :
she was asking herself if the Nuns at the old
moated house ever opened their doors to
women, whose one claim on their common
Christianity was the claim to be pitied—

when she heard Linley's footsteps approaching her door.

His tone was kind; his manner was gentle; his tender interest in her seemed to have revived. Her long absence had alarmed him; he feared she might be ill. "I was only thinking," she said. He smiled, and sat down by her, and asked if she had been thinking of the place that they should go to when they left London.

CHAPTER XXXIII.

MRS. ROMSEY.

THE one hotel at Sandyseal was full, from the topmost story to the ground floor ; and by far the larger half of the landlord's guests were invalids sent to him by the doctors.

To persons of excitable temperament, in search of amusement, the place offered no attractions. Situated at the innermost end of a dull little bay, Sandyseal—so far as any view of the shipping in the Channel was concerned—might have been built on a remote island in the Pacific Ocean. Vessels of any importance kept well out of the way

of treacherous shoals and currents, lurking
at the entrance of the bay. The anchorage
ground was good; but the depth of water
was suited to small vessels only—to shabby
old fishing-smacks which seldom paid their
expenses, and to dirty little coasters carrying
coals and potatoes. At the back of the
hotel, two slovenly rows of cottages took
their crooked course inland. Sailing masters
of yachts, off duty, sat and yawned at the
windows; lazy fishermen looked wearily at
the weather over their garden gates; and
superfluous coastguards gathered together
in a wooden observatory, and levelled
useless telescopes at an empty sea. The
flat open country, with its few dwarf trees
and its mangy hedges, lay prostrate under
the sky in all the desolation of solitary
space, and left the famous restorative air
free to build up dilapidated nerves, without
an object to hinder its passage at any point

33—2

of the compass. The lonely drab-coloured road that led to the nearest town offered to visitors, taking airings, a view of a low brown object in the distance, said to be the convent in which the Nuns lived, secluded from mortal eyes. At one side of the hotel, the windows looked on a little wooden pier, sadly in want of repair. On the other side, a walled enclosure accommodated yachts of light tonnage, stripped of their rigging, and sitting solitary on a bank of mud until their owners wanted them. In this neighbourhood there was a small outlying colony of shops : one that sold fruit and fish ; one that dealt in groceries and tobacco ; one shut up, with a bill in the window inviting a tenant ; and one, behind the Methodist Chapel, answering the double purpose of a post-office and a store-house for ropes and coals. Beyond these objects there was nothing (and this was the great. charm of

the place) to distract the attention of invalids, following the doctor's directions, and
from morning to night taking care of their
health.

The time was evening ; the scene was
one of the private sitting-rooms in the
hotel ; and the purpose in view was a little
tea-party.

Rich Mrs. Romsey, connected with
commerce as wife of the chief partner in the
firm of Romsey and Renshaw, was staying
at the hotel in the interests of her three
children. They were of delicate constitution ;
their complete recovery, after severe illness
which had passed from one to the other, was
less speedy than had been anticipated ; and
the doctor had declared that the nervous
system was, in each case, more or less in
need of repair. To arrive at this conclusion, and to recommend a visit to Sandy-

seal, were events which followed each other (medically speaking) as a matter of course.

The health of the children had greatly improved ; the famous air had agreed with them, and the discovery of new playfellows had agreed with them. They had made acquaintance with Lady Myrie's well-bred boys, and with Mrs. Norman's charming little Kitty. The most cordial good-feeling had established itself among the mothers. Owing a return for hospitalities received from Lady Myrie and Mrs. Norman, Mrs. Romsey had invited the two ladies to drink tea with her in honour of an interesting domestic event. Her husband, absent on the Continent for some time past, on business connected with his firm, had returned to England, and had that evening joined his wife and children at Sandyseal.

Lady Myrie had arrived, and Mr. Romsey had been presented to her. Mrs. Norman, expected to follow, was represented by a courteous note of apology. She was not well that evening, and she begged to be excused.

"This is a great disappointment," Mrs. Romsey said to her husband. "You would have been charmed with Mrs. Norman— highly-bred, accomplished, a perfect lady. And she leaves us to-morrow. The departure will not be an early one; and I shall find an opportunity, my dear, of introducing you to my friend and her sweet little Kitty."

Mr. Romsey looked interested for a moment, when he first heard Mrs. Norman's name. After that, he slowly stirred his tea, and seemed to be thinking, instead of listening to his wife.

"Have you made the lady's acquaintance here?" he inquired.

"Yes—and I hope I have made a friend

for life," Mrs. Romsey said with enthu-
siasm.

"And so do I," Lady Myrie added.

Mr. Romsey went on with his inquiries.

"Is she a handsome woman ?"

Both the ladies answered the question
together.   Lady Myrie described Mrs.
Norman, in one dreadful word, as " Clas-
sical."   By comparison with this, Mrs.
Romsey's reply was intelligible.   " Not
even illness can spoil her beauty !"

" Including the headache she has got to-
night?" Mr. Romsey suggested.

" Don't be ill-natured, dear !   Mrs.
Norman is here by the advice of one of the
first physicians in London : she has suffered
under serious troubles, poor thing."

Mr. Romsey persisted in being ill-natured.
" Connected with her husband?" he asked.

Lady Myrie entered a protest.   She was
a widow; and it was notorious among her

friends, that the death of her husband had been the happiest event in her married life. But she understood her duty to herself as a respectable woman. " I think, Mr. Romsey, you might have spared that cruel allusion," she said with dignity.

Mr. Romsey apologized. He had his reasons for wishing to know something more about Mrs. Norman; he proposed to withdraw his last remark, and to put his inquiries under another form. Might he ask his wife if anybody had seen *Mr.* Norman?

" No."

" Or heard of him?"

Mrs. Romsey answered in the negative once more, and added a question on her own account. What did all this mean?

" It means," Lady Myrie interposed, " what we poor women are all exposed to— scandal." She had not yet forgiven Mr.

Romsey's allusion, and she looked at him pointedly as she spoke. There are some impenetrable men on whom looks produce no impression. Mr. Romsey was one of them. He turned to his wife, and said quietly, "What I mean is, that I know more of Mrs. Norman than you do. I have heard of her—never mind how or where. She is a lady who has been celebrated in the newspapers. Don't be alarmed. She is no less a person than the divorced Mrs. Linley."

The two ladies looked at each other in blank dismay. Restrained by a sense of conjugal duty, Mrs. Romsey only indulged in an exclamation. Lady Myrie, independent of restraint, expressed her opinion, and said, "Quite impossible!"

"The Mrs. Norman whom I mean,' Mr. Romsey went on, "has, as I have been told, a mother living. The old lady has been twice married. Her name is Mrs. Presty."

This settled the question. Mrs. Presty was established, in her own proper person, with her daughter and grandchild at the hotel. Lady Myrie yielded to the force of evidence; she lifted her hands in horror : " This is too dreadful!"

Mrs. Romsey took a more compassionate view of the disclosure. " Surely the poor lady is to be pitied?" she gently suggested.

Lady Myrie looked at her friend in astonishment. " My dear, you must have forgotten what the Judge said about her. Surely you read the report of the case in the newspapers?"

" No; I heard of the trial, and that's all. What did the Judge say?"

" Say?" Lady Myrie repeated. " What did he not say! His lordship declared that he had a great mind not to grant the Divorce at all. He spoke of this dreadful woman who has deceived us, in the severest terms ; he said she had behaved in a most improper manner. She had encouraged the abominable governess ; and if her husband had yielded to temptation, it was her fault. And more besides, that I don't remember."

Mr. Romsey's wife appealed to him in despair. "What am I to do?" she asked helplessly.

"Do nothing," was the wise reply. "Didn't you say she was going away to-morrow?"

"That's the worst of it!" Mrs. Romsey declared. "Her little girl Kitty gives a farewell dinner to-morrow to our children; and I've promised to take them to say good-bye."

Lady Myrie pronounced sentence without hesitation. "Of course your girls mustn't go. Daughters! Think of their reputations when they grow up!"

"Are you in the same scrape with my wife?" Mr. Romsey asked.

Lady Myrie corrected his language. "I have been deceived in the same way," she said. "Though my children are boys (which perhaps makes a difference) I feel it my duty as a mother not to let them get into bad company. I do nothing myself in an underhand way. No excuses! I shall send a note, and tell Mrs. Norman why she doesn't see my boys to-morrow."

"Isn't that a little hard on her?" said merciful Mrs. Romsey.

Mr. Romsey agreed with his wife, on grounds of expediency. "Never make a row if you can help it," was the peaceable principle to which this gentleman committed himself. " Send word that the

children have caught colds, and get over it
in that way."

Mrs. Romsey looked gratefully at her
admirable husband. "Just the thing!"
she said, with an air of relief.

Lady Myrie's sense of duty expressed
itself with the strictest adherence to the
laws of courtesy. She rose, smiled re-
signedly, and said "Good-night."

Almost at the same moment, innocent
little Kitty astonished her mother and
her grandmother by appearing before them
in her night-gown, after she had been put
to bed nearly two hours since.

"What will this child do next!" Mrs.
Presty exclaimed.

Kitty told the truth. "I can't go to
sleep, Grandmamma."

"Why not, my darling?" her mother
asked.

" I'm so excited, Mamma."

" About what, Kitty?"

" About my dinner-party to-morrow. Oh," said the child, clasping her hands earnestly as she thought of her playfellows, " I do so hope it will go off well!"

CHAPTER XXXIV.

MRS. PRESTY.

BELONGING to the elder generation which
has lived to see the Age of Hurry, and has
no sympathy with it, Mrs. Presty entered
the sitting-room at the hotel, two hours
before the time that had been fixed for
leaving Sandyseal, with her mind at ease on
the subject of her luggage. " My boxes
are locked, strapped, and labelled ; I hate
being hurried. What's that you're reading?" she asked, discovering a book on
her daughter's lap, and a hasty action on
her daughter's part, which looked like
trying to hide it.

Mrs. Norman made the most common, and—where the object is to baffle curiosity—the most useless of prevaricating replies. When her mother asked her what she was reading she answered : "Nothing."

"Nothing!" Mrs. Presty repeated with an ironical assumption of interest. "The work of all others, Catherine, that I most want to read." She snatched up the book ; opened it at the first page, and discovered an inscription in faded ink which roused her indignation. "To dear Catherine, from Herbert, on the anniversary of our marriage." What unintended mockery in those words, read by the later light of the Divorce ! "Well, this *is* mean," said Mrs. Presty. "Keeping that wretch's present, after the public exposure which he has forced on you. Oh, Catherine!"

Catherine was not quite so patient with her mother as usual. "Keeping my best remembrance of the happy time of my life," she answered.

. " Misplaced sentiment," Mrs. Presty declared ; " I shall put the book out of the way. Your brain is softening, my dear, under the influence of this stupefying place."

Catherine asserted her own opinion against her mother's opinion, for the second time. " I have recovered my health at Sandyseal," she said. " I like the place, and I am sorry to leave it."

" Give me the shop windows, the streets, the life, the racket, and the smoke of London," cried Mrs. Presty. " Thank Heaven, these rooms are let over our heads, and out we must go, whether we like it or not."

This expression of gratitude was followed by a knock at the door, and by a voice outside asking leave to come in, which was, beyond all doubt, the voice of Randal Linley. With Catherine's book still in her possession, Mrs. Presty opened the table-drawer, threw it in, and closed the drawer with a bang. Discovering the two ladies, Randal stopped in the doorway, and stared at them in astonishment.

. " Didn't you expect to see us?" Mrs. Presty inquired.

"I heard you were here, from our friend Sarrazin," Randal said; " but I expected to see Captain Bennydeck. Have I mistaken the number? Surely these are his rooms?"

Catherine attempted to explain. " They *were* Captain Bennydeck's rooms," she began; " but he was so kind, although we are perfect strangers to him——"

Mrs. Presty interposed. " My dear Catherine, you have not had my advantages; you have not been taught to make a complicated statement in few words. Permit

34—2

me to seize the points (in the late Mr. Presty's style), and to put them in the strongest light. This place, Randal, is always full ; and we didn't write long enough beforehand to secure rooms. Captain Bennydeck happened to be downstairs when he heard that we were obliged to go away, ¬and that one of us was a lady in delicate health. This sweetest of men sent us word that we were welcome to take his rooms, and that he would sleep on board his yacht. Conduct worthy of Sir Charles Grandison himself. When I went downstairs to thank him, he was gone—and here we have been for nearly three weeks; sometimes seeing the captain's yacht, but, to our great surprise, never seeing the captain himself."

" There's nothing to be surprised at, Mrs. Presty. Captain Bennydeck likes doing kind things, and hates being thanked for it.

I expected him to meet me here to-day."

Catherine went to the window. " He is coming to meet you," she said. " There is his yacht in the bay."

" And in a dead calm," Randal added, joining her. " The vessel will not get here, before I am obliged to go away again."

Catherine looked at him timidly. "Do I drive you away?" she asked, in tones that faltered a little.

Randal wondered what she could possibly be thinking of, and acknowledged it in so many words.

" She is thinking of the Divorce," Mrs. Presty explained. " You have heard of it, of course; and perhaps you take your brother's part?"

"I do nothing of the sort, ma'am. My brother has been in the wrong from first to last." He turned to Catherine. " I will stay with you, as long as I can, with the greatest pleasure," he said earnestly and kindly. "The truth is, I am on my way to visit some friends; and if Captain Benny-deck had got here in time to see me, I must have gone away to the junction to catch the next train westward, just as I am going now. I had only two words to say to the Captain; about a person in whom he is inter-ested—and I can say them in this way." He wrote in pencil on one of his visiting cards, and laid it on the table. " I shall be back in London, in a week," he resumed, "and you will tell me at what address I can find you. In the meanwhile, I miss Kitty. Where is she?"

Kitty was sent for. She entered the room looking unusually quiet and sub-dued — but, discovering Randal, became herself again in a moment, and jumped on his knee.

" Oh, Uncle Randal, I'm so glad to see you!" She checked herself, and looked at her mother. "May I call him Uncle Randal?" she asked. "Or has *he* changed his name too?"

Mrs. Presty shook a warning forefinger at her granddaughter, and reminded Kitty that she had been told not to talk about names. Randal saw the child's look of bewilderment, and felt for her. "She may talk as she pleases to me," he said, "but not to strangers. She understands that, I am sure."

Kitty laid her cheek fondly against her Uncle's cheek. "Everything is changed," she whispered. "We travel about; Papa has left us, and Syd has left us, and we have got a new name. We are Norman now. I wish I was grown up, and old enough to understand it."

Randal tried to reconcile her to her

own happy ignorance. "You have got your dear good mother," he said, "and you have got me, and you have got your toys——"

"And some nice boys and girls to play with," cried Kitty, eagerly following the new suggestion. "They are all coming here directly to dine with me. You will stay and have dinner too, won't you?"

Randal promised to dine with Kitty when they met in London. Before he left the room he pointed to his card on the table. "Let my friend see that message," he said, as he went out.

The moment the door had closed on him, Mrs. Presty startled her daughter by taking up the card and looking at what Randal had written on it. "It isn't a letter, Catherine; and you know how superior I am to common prejudices." With that

defence of her proceeding, she coolly read
the message :

"I am sorry to say that I can tell you
nothing more of your old friend's daughter
as yet. I can only repeat that she neither
needs nor deserves the help that you kindly
offer to her."

Mrs. Presty laid the card down again,
and owned that she wished Randal had
been a little more explicit. "Who can
it be?" she wondered. "Another young
hussey gone wrong?"

Kitty turned to her mother with a look
of alarm. "What's a hussey?" she asked.
"Does Grandmamma mean me?" The
great hotel clock in the hall struck two,
and the child's anxieties took a new direction. "Isn't it time my little friends came
to see me?" she said.

It was half an hour past the time.
Catherine proposed to send to Lady Myrie
and Mrs. Romsey, and inquire if anything
had happened to cause the delay. As she
told Kitty to ring the bell, the waiter came
in with two letters, addressed to Mrs.
Norman.

Mrs. Presty had her own ideas, and drew
her own conclusions. She watched Catherine attentively. Even Kitty observed that
her mother's face grew paler and paler as
she read the letters. " You look as if
you were frightened, Mamma." There
was no reply. Kitty began to feel so
uneasy on the subject of her dinner and
her guests, that she actually ventured on
putting a question to her Grandmother.

" Will they be long, do you think, before
they come?" she asked.

The old lady's worldly wisdom had
passed, by this time, from a state of sus-

picion to a state of certainty. "My child,"
she answered, "they won't come at all."

Kitty ran to her mother, eager to inquire
if what Mrs. Presty had told her could
possibly be true. Before a word had passed
her lips, she shrank back, too frightened to
speak.

Never, in her little experience, had she
been startled by such a look in her mother's
face as the look that confronted her now.
For the first time, Catherine saw her child
trembling at the sight of her. Before that
discovery, the emotions that shook her
under the insult which she had received,
lost their hold. She caught Kitty up in
her arms. "My darling, my angel, it isn't
you I am thinking of. I love you!—I
love you! In the whole world there isn't
such a good child, such a sweet, loveable,
pretty child as you are. Oh, how disappointed she looks—she's crying. Don't

break my heart!—don't cry!" Kitty held
up her head, and cleared her eyes with a
dash of her hand. "I won't cry, Mamma."
And child as she was, she was as good as
her word. Her mother looked at her, and
burst into tears.

Perversely reluctant, the better nature
that was in Mrs. Presty rose to the surface,
forced to show itself. "Cry, Catherine,"
she said, kindly; "it will do you good.
Leave the child to me."

With a gentleness that astonished Kitty,
she led her little granddaughter to the
window, and pointed to the public walk in
front of the house. "I know what will
comfort you," the wise old woman began;
"look out of the window." Kitty obeyed.

"I don't see my little friends coming,"
she said. Mrs. Presty still pointed to some
object on the public walk. "That's better
than nothing, isn't it?" she persisted.

" Come with me to the maid ; she shall go with you, and take care of you." Kitty whispered, " May I give Mamma a kiss first!" Sensible Mrs. Presty delayed the kiss for awhile. " Wait till you come back, and then you can tell your Mamma what a treat you have had." Arrived at the door on their way out, Kitty whispered again : " I want to say something."—" Well, what is it ?"—" Will you tell the donkey-boy to make him gallop ?"—" I'll tell the boy he shall have sixpence if you are satisfied; and you will see what he does then." Kitty looked up earnestly in her Grandmother's face. " What a pity it is you are not always like what you are now!" she said. Mrs. Presty actually blushed.

CHAPTER XXXV.

CAPTAIN BENNYDECK.

For some time, Catherine and her mother had been left together undisturbed.

Mrs. Presty had read (and destroyed) the letters of Lady Myrie and Mrs. Romsey, with the most unfeigned contempt for the writers—had repeated what the Judge had really said, as distinguished from Lady Myrie's malicious version of it—and had expressed her intention of giving Catherine a word of advice, when she was sufficiently composed to profit by it. " You have recovered your good looks, after that fit of crying," Mrs. Presty admitted, " but not your good spirits. What is worrying you now ?"

" I can't help thinking of poor Kitty."

" My dear, the child wants nobody's pity. She's blowing away all her troubles by a ride in the fresh air, on the favourite donkey that she feeds every morning. Yes, yes, you needn't tell me you are in a false position ; and nobody can deny that it's shameful to make the child feel it. Now listen to me. Properly understood, those two spiteful women have done you a kindness. They have as good as told you how to protect yourself in the time to come. Deceive the vile world, Catherine, as it deserves to be deceived. Shelter yourself behind a respectable character that will spare you these insults in the future." In the energy of her conviction, Mrs. Presty struck her fist on the table, and finished in three audacious words : " Be a Widow !"

It was plainly said—and yet Catherine seemed to be at a loss to understand what her mother meant.

"Don't doubt about it," Mrs. Presty went on; "do it. Think of Kitty if you won't think of yourself. In a few years more she will be a young lady. She may have an offer of marriage which may be everything we desire. Suppose her sweetheart's family is a religious family; and suppose your Divorce, and the Judge's remarks on it, are discovered. What will happen then?"

"Is it possible that you are in earnest?" Catherine asked. "Have you seriously thought of the advice that you are giving me? Setting aside the deceit, you know as well as I do that Kitty would ask questions. Do you think I can tell my child that her father is dead? A lie—and such a dreadful lie as that?"

"Nonsense!" said Mrs. Presty.

" Nonsense ?" Catherine repeated in-dignantly.

"'Rank nonsense," her mother persisted. " Hasn't your situation forced you to lie already ? When the child asks why her father and her governess have left us, haven't you been obliged to invent excuses which are lies ? If the man who was once your husband isn't as good as dead to *you,* I should like to know what your Divorce means! My poor dear, do you think you can go on as you are going on now ? How many thousands of people have read the newspaper account of the trial ? How many hundreds of people—interested in a handsome woman like you—will wonder why they never see Mr. Norman ? What? You will go abroad again ? Go where you may, you will attract attention; you will make an enemy of every ugly woman who looks at you. Strain at a gnat, Catherine, and swallow a camel. It's only a question of time. Sooner or later you will find yourself driven to it; you will be a Widow. Here's the waiter again. What does the man want now?"

The waiter answered by announcing:

" Captain Bennydeck."

Catherine's mother was nearer to the door than Catherine; she attracted the Captain's attention first. He addressed his apologies to her: "Pray excuse me for disturbing you——"

Mrs. Presty had an eye for a handsome man, irrespective of what his age might be. In the language of the conjurors, a " magic change" appeared in her; she became brightly agreeable in a moment.

"Oh, Captain Bennydeck, you mustn't make excuses for coming into your own room!"

Captain Bennydeck went on with his

excuses nevertheless. "The landlady tells me that I have unluckily missed seeing Mr. Randal Linley, and that he has left a message for me. I shouldn't otherwise have ventured——"

Mrs. Presty stopped him once more. The Captain's claim to the Captain's rooms was the principle on which she took her stand. She revived the irresistible smiles which had conquered Mr. Norman and Mr. Presty. "No ceremony, I beg and pray! You are at home here—take the easy-chair!"

Catherine advanced a few steps; it was time to stop her mother, if the thing could be done. She felt just embarrassment enough to heighten her colour, and to show her beauty to the greatest advantage. It literally staggered the Captain, the moment he looked at her. His customary composure, as a well-bred man, deserted him; he bowed confusedly; he had not a word to say. Mrs. Presty seized her opportunity, and introduced them to each other. My daughter Mrs. Norman—Captain Benny-deck." Compassionating him, under the impression that he was a shy man, Catherine tried to set him at his ease. "I am indeed glad to have an opportunity of thanking you," she said, inviting him by a gesture to be seated. "In this delightful air, I have recovered my health, and I owe it to your kindness."

The Captain regained his self-possession. Expressions of gratitude had been addressed to him which, in his modest estimate of himself, he could not feel that he had deserved.

"You little know," he replied, "under what interested motives I have acted. When I established myself in this hotel, I was fairly driven out of my yacht by a guest who went sailing with me."

Mrs. Presty became deeply interested. " Dear me, what did he do ?"

Captain Bennydeck answered gravely : " He snored."

Catherine was amused ; Mrs. Presty burst out laughing ; the Captain's dry humour asserted itself as quaintly as ever. " This is no laughing matter," he resumed, looking at Catherine. " My vessel is a small one. For two nights the awful music of my friend's nose kept me sleepless. When I woke him, and said, ' Don't snore,' he apologised in the sweetest manner, and began again. On the third day I anchored in the bay here, determined to get a night's rest on shore. A dispute about the price of these rooms offered them to me. I sent a note of apology on board—and slept peacefully. The next morning, my sailing master informed me that there had been, what he called, ' a little swell in the night.'

He reported the sounds made by my friend on this occasion to have been the awful sounds of sea-sickness. ' The gentleman left the yacht, sir, the first thing this morning,' he said ; ' and he's gone home by railway.' On the day when you happened to arrive, my cabin was my own again ; and I can honestly thank you for relieving me of my rooms. Do you make a long stay here, Mrs. Norman ?"

Catherine answered that they were going to London by the next train. Seeing Randal's card still unnoticed on the table, she handed it to the Captain.

"Is Mr. Linley an old friend of yours ?" he asked, as he took the card.

Mrs. Presty hastened to answer in the affirmative for her daughter. It was plain that Randal had discreetly abstained from mentioning his true connection with them. Would he preserve the same silence if the

Captain spoke of his visit to Mrs. Norman, when he and his friend met next ? Mrs. Presty's mind might have been at ease on that subject, if she had known how to appreciate Randal's character and Randal's motives. The same keen sense of the family disgrace, which had led him to conceal from Captain Bennydeck his brother's illicit relations with Sydney Westerfield, had compelled him to keep secret his former association, as brother-in-law, with the divorced wife. Her change of name had hitherto protected her from discovery by the Captain, and would in all probability continue to protect her in the future. The good Bennydeck had been enjoying himself at sea, when the Divorce was granted, and when the newspapers reported the proceedings. He rarely went to his club, and he never associated with persons of either sex to whom gossip and scandal are as the breath of their lives. Ignorant of these circumstances, and remembering what had happened on that day, Mrs. Presty looked at him with some anxiety on her daughter's account, while he was reading the message on Randal's card. There was little to see. His fine face expressed a quiet sorrow, and he sighed as he put the card back in his pocket.

An interval of silence followed. Captain Bennydeck was thinking over the message which he had just read. Catherine and her mother were looking at him with the same interest, inspired by very different motives. The interview so pleasantly begun was in some danger of lapsing into formality and embarrassment, when a new personage appeared on the scene.

Kitty had returned in triumph from her ride. "Mamma! the donkey did more than gallop—he kicked, and I fell off. Oh, I'm not hurt!" cried the child, seeing the alarm in her mother's face. "Tumbling off is such a funny sensation. It isn't as if you fell on the ground; it's as if the ground came up to *you* and said—Bump!" She had got as far as that, when the progress of her narrative was suspended by the discovery of a strange gentleman in the room.

The smile that brightened the captain's face, when Kitty opened the door, answered for him as a man who loved children. " Your little girl, Mrs. Norman ?" he said.

" Yes."

(A common question and a common reply. Nothing worth noticing, in either the one or the other, at the time—and yet they proved to be important enough to turn Catherine's life into a new course.)

In the meanwhile, Kitty had been whispering to her mother. She wanted to know the strange gentleman's name. The Captain heard her. "My name is Bennydeck," he said ; "will you come to me ?"

Kitty had heard the name mentioned in connection with a yacht. Like all children, she knew a friend the moment she looked at him. "I've seen your pretty boat, sir," she said, crossing the room to Captain Benny-deck. "Is it very nice when you go sailing ?"

"If you were not going back to London, my dear, I should ask your Mamma to let me take you sailing with me. Perhaps we shall have another opportunity."

The Captain's answer delighted Kitty. "Oh, yes, to-morrow or next day!" she suggested. "Do you know where to find me in London ? Mamma, where do I live, when I am in London ?" Before her mother could answer, she hit on a new idea. "Don't tell me ; I'll find it for myself. It's on Grandmamma's boxes, and they're in the passage."

Captain Bennydeck's eyes followed her, as she left the room, with an expression of interest which more than confirmed the favourable impression that he had already produced on Catherine. She was on the point of asking if he was married, and had children of his own, when Kitty came back, and declared the right address to be Buck's Hotel, Sydenham. "Mamma puts things down for fear of forgetting them," she added. "Will you put down Buck?"

The Captain took out his pocket-book, and appealed pleasantly to Mrs. Norman. "May I follow your example?" he asked. Catherine not only humoured the little joke, but, gratefully remembering his kindness, said : "Don't forget, when you are in London, that Kitty's invitation is my invitation, too." At the same moment, punc-

tual Mrs. Presty looked at her watch, and
reminded her daughter that railways were
not in the habit of allowing passengers to
keep them waiting.   Catherine rose, and
gave her hand to the Captain at parting.
Kitty improved on her mother's form of
farewell ; she gave him a kiss, and whispered
a little reminder of her own : " There's a
river in London—don't forget your boat."

Captain Bennydeck opened the door for
them, secretly wishing that he could follow
Mrs. Norman to the station and travel by
the same train.

Mrs. Presty made no attempt to remind
him that she was still in the room.   Where
her family interests were concerned, the old
lady was capable (on very slight encouragement) of looking a long way into the future.
She was looking into the future now.   The
Captain's social position was all that could be
desired ; he was evidently in easy pecuniary

circumstances ; he admired Catherine and Catherine's child. If he only proved to be a single man, Mrs. Presty's prophetic soul, without waiting an instant to reflect, perceived a dazzling future. Captain Bennydeck approached to take leave. "Not just yet," pleaded the most agreeable of women ; "my luggage was ready two hours ago. Sit down again for a few minutes. You seem to like my little granddaughter.

"If I had such a child as that," the Captain answered, "I believe I should be the happiest man living."

"Ah, my dear sir, all isn't gold that glitters," Mrs. Presty remarked. "That proverb must have been originally intended to apply to children. May I presume to make you the subject of a guess ? I fancy you are not a married man."

The Captain looked a little surprised.

"You are quite right," he said; "I have never been married."

At a later period, Mrs. Presty owned that she felt an inclination to reward him for confessing himself to be a bachelor, by a kiss. He innocently checked that impulse by putting a question. "Had you any particular reason," he asked, "for guessing that I was a single man?"

Mrs. Presty modestly acknowledged that she had only her own experience to help her. "You wouldn't be quite so fond of other people's children," she said, "if you were a married man. Ah, your time will come yet—I mean your wife will come."

He answered this sadly. "My time has gone by. I have never had the opportunities that have been granted to some favoured men." He thought of the favoured man who had married Mrs. Norman. Was her husband worthy of his happiness? "Is

would have been pretty, if she had not looked ill and out of spirits. What would he have said, what would he have done, if he had known that those two strangers were Randal Linley's brother, and Roderick Westerfield's daughter?

CHAPTER XXXVI.

MR. AND MRS. HERBERT.

THE stealthy influence of distrust fastens its
hold on the mind by slow degrees. Little
by little it reaches its fatal end, and dis-
guises delusion successfully under the garb
of truth.

Day after day, the false conviction grew
on Sydney's mind that Herbert Linley was
comparing the life he led now with the
happier life which he remembered at Mount
Morven. Day after day, her unreasoning
fear contemplated the time when Herbert
Linley would leave her friendless, in a
world that had no place in it for women

like herself. Delusion—fatal delusion that
looked like truth! Morally weak as he
might be, the man whom she feared to trust
had not yet entirely lost the sense which
birth and breeding had firmly fastened in
him—the sense of honour. Acting under
that influence, he was (if the expression
may be permitted) consistent even in incon-
sistency. With equal sincerity of feeling,
he reproached himself for his infidelity
towards the woman whom he had deserted,
and devoted himself to his duty towards
the woman whom he had misled. In
Sydney's presence — suffer as he might
under the struggle to maintain his resolution when he was alone—he kept his inter-
course with her studiously gentle in manner,
and considerate in language; his conduct
offered assurances for the future which she
could only see through the falsifying medium
of her own distrust.

In the delusion that now possessed her, she read, over and over again, the letter which Captain Bennydeck had addressed to her father ; she saw, more and more clearly, the circumstances which associated her situation with the situation of the poor girl who had closed her wasted life among the nuns in the French convent.

Two results followed on this state of things.

When Herbert asked to what part of England they should go, on leaving London, she mentioned Sandyseal as a place that she had heard of, and felt some curiosity to see. The same day—bent on pleasing her ; careless where he lived now, at home or abroad—he wrote to engage rooms at the hotel.

A time followed, during which they were obliged to wait until rooms were free. In this interval, brooding over the melancholy absence of friend or relative in whom she could confide, her morbid dread of the future decided her on completing the parallel between herself and that other lost creature of whom she had read. Sydney opened communications anonymously with the Benedictine community at Sandyseal.

She addressed the Mother Superior; telling the truth about herself with but one concealment, the concealment of names. She revealed her isolated position among her fellow creatures; she declared her fervent desire to repent of her wickedness, and to lead a religious life; she acknowledged her misfortune in having been brought up by persons careless of religion, and she confessed to having attended a Protestant place of worship, as a mere matter of form connected with the duties of a teacher at a school. " The religion of any Christian woman who will help me to be more like herself," she wrote, " is the religion to which I am willing and eager to belong. If I come to you in my distress, will you receive me?" To that simple appeal, she added a request that an answer might be addressed to " S. W., Post-office, Sandyseal."

When Captain Bennydeck and Sydney Westerfield passed each other as strangers, in the hall of the hotel, that letter had been posted in London a week since.

The servant showed "Mr. and Mrs. Herbert" into their sitting - room, and begged that they would be so good as to wait a few minutes, while the other rooms were being prepared for them.

Sydney seated herself in silence. She was thinking of her letter, and wondering whether a reply was waiting for her at the Post-office.

Moving towards the window to look at the view, Herbert paused to examine some prints hanging on the walls, which were superior as works of art to the customary decorations of a room at an hotel. If he had gone straight to the window he might have seen his divorced wife, his child, and his wife's mother, getting into the carriage which took them to the railway station.

" Come, Sydney," he said, " and look at the sea."

She joined him wearily, with a faint smile. It was a calm sunny day. Bathing machines were on the beach ; children were playing here and there ; and white sails of pleasure boats were visible in the offing. The dullness of Sandyseal wore a quiet homely aspect which was pleasant to the eyes of strangers. Sydney said absently, "I think I shall like the place." And Herbert added, " Let us hope that the air

will make you feel stronger." He meant
it and said it kindly—but, instead of
looking at her while he spoke, he continued
to look at the view. A woman sure of her
position would not have allowed this trifling
circumstance, even if she had observed it, to
disturb her. Sydney thought of the day
in London when he had persisted in looking
out at the street, and returned in silence to
her chair.

Had he been so unfortunate as to offend
her? And in what way? As that doubt
occurred to Herbert his mind turned to
Catherine. *She* never took offence at trifles;
a word of kindness from him, no matter
how unimportant it might be, always
claimed affectionate acknowledgment in the
days when he was living with his wife. In
another moment he had dismissed that
remembrance, and could trust himself to
return to Sydney.

" If you find that Sandyseal confirms your first impression," he said, " let me know it in time, so that I may make arrangements for a longer stay. I have only taken the rooms here for a fortnight."

" Thank you, Herbert; I think a fort-night will be long enough."

" Long enough for you?" he asked.

Her morbid sensitiveness mistook him again; she fancied there was an undernote of irony in his tone.

" Long enough for both of us," she replied.

He drew a chair to her side. " Do you take it for granted," he said smiling, " that I shall get tired of the place first ?"

She shrank, poor creature, even from his smile. There was, as she thought, some-thing contemptuous in the good-humour of it.

" We have been to many places,' she

reminded him, "and we have got tired of them together."

" Is that my fault?"

" I didn't say it was."

He got up and approached the bell. " I think the journey has a little over-tired you," he resumed. " Would you like to go to your room?"

" I will go to my room, if you wish it."

He waited a little, and answered her as quietly as ever. " What I really wish," he said, " is that we had consulted a doctor while we were in London. You seem to be very easily irritated of late. I observe a change in you, which I willingly attribute to the state of your health——"

She interrupted him. " What change do you mean?"

"It's quite possible I may be mistaken, Sydney. But I have more than once, as I think, seen something in your manner which suggests that you distrust me."

"I distrust the evil life we are leading," she burst out, "and I see the end of it coming. Oh, I don't blame you! You are kind and considerate, you do your best to hide it; but you have lived long enough with me to regret the woman whom you have lost. You begin to feel the sacrifice you have made—and no wonder. Say the word, Herbert, and I release you."

"I will never say the word!"

She hesitated—first inclined, then afraid, to believe him. "I have grace enough left in me," she went on, "to feel the bitterest repentance for the wrong that I have done to Mrs. Linley. When it ends, as it must end, in our parting, will you ask your wife—— ?"

Even his patience began to fail him; he refused — firmly, not angrily — to hear

more. "She is no longer my wife,"
said.

Sydney's bitterness and Sydney's penitence were mingled, as opposite emotions
only *can* be mingled in a woman's breast.
"Will you ask your wife to forgive you?"
she persisted.

"After we have been divorced at her
petition?" He pointed to the window as
he said it. "Look at the sea. If I was
drowning out yonder, I might as well ask
the sea to forgive me."

He produced no effect on her. She
ignored the Divorce ; her passionate
remorse asserted itself as obstinately as
ever. "Mrs. Linley is a good woman,"
she insisted; "Mrs. Linley is a Christian
woman."

"I have lost all claim on her—even the
claim to remember her virtues," he answered
sternly. "No more of it, Sydney! I am

sorry I have disappointed you ; I am sorry if you are weary of me."

At those last words her manner changed. "Wound me as cruelly as you please," she said humbly. "I will try to bear it."

"I wouldn't wound you for the world! Why do you persist in distressing me? Why do you feel suspicion of me which I have not deserved?" He stopped, and held out his hand. "Don't let us quarrel, Sydney. Which will you do? Keep your bad opinion of me, or give me a fair trial?"

She loved him so dearly ; she was so young—and the young are so ready to hope! Still, she struggled against herself. "Herbert! is it your pity for me that is speaking now?"

He left her in despair. "It's useless!" he said sadly. "Nothing will conquer your inveterate distrust."

She followed him. With a faint cry of entreaty she made him turn to her, and held him in a trembling embrace, and rested her head on his bosom. "Forgive me—be patient with me—love me." That was all she could say.

He attempted to calm her agitation by speaking lightly. "At last, Sydney, we are friends again!" he said.

Friends? All the woman in her recoiled from that insufficient word. "Are we Lovers?" she whispered.

"Yes!"

With that assurance her anxious heart was content. She smiled; she looked out at the sea with a new appreciation of the view. "The air of this place will do me good now," she said. "Are my eyes red, Herbert? Let me go and bathe them, and make myself fit to be seen."

She rang the bell. The chambermaid

answered it, ready to show the other rooms. She turned round at the door.

" Let's try to make our sitting-room look like home," she suggested. " How dismal, how dreadfully like a thing that doesn't belong to us, that empty table looks ! Put some of your books and my keepsakes on it, while I am away. I'll bring my work with me when I come back."

He had left his travellers' bag on a chair, when he first came in. Now that he was alone, and under no restraint, he sighed as he unlocked the bag. " Home?" he repeated: " we have no home. Poor girl ! poor unhappy girl ! Let me help her to deceive herself."

He opened the bag. The little fragile presents, which she called her " keepsakes," had been placed by her own hands in the upper part of the bag, so that the books should not weigh on them, and had been

carefully protected by wrappings of cott
wool. Taking them out, one by one,
Herbert found a delicate china candlestick
(intended to hold a wax-taper) broken into
two pieces, in spite of the care that had been
taken to preserve it. Of no great value in
itself, old associations made the candlestick
precious to Sydney. It had been broken at
the stem, and could be easily mended so as
to keep the accident concealed. Consulting
the waiter, Herbert discovered that the
fracture could be repaired at the nearest
town, and that the place would be within
reach when he went out for a walk. In
fear of another disaster, if he put it back in
the bag, he opened a drawer in the table,
and laid the two fragments carefully inside,
at the further end. In doing this, his hand
touched something that had been already
placed in the drawer. He drew it out, and
found that it was a book—the same book

that Mrs. Presty (surely the evil genius of the family again!) had hidden from Randal's notice, and had forgotten when she left the hotel.

Herbert instantly recognised the gilding on the cover, imitated from a design invented by himself. He remembered the inscription, and yet he read it again :

" To dear Catherine from Herbert, on the anniversary of our marriage."

The book dropped from his hand on the table, as if it had been a new discovery, torturing him with a new pain.

His wife (he persisted in thinking of her as his wife) must have occupied the room— might perhaps have been the person whom he had succeeded, as a guest at the hotel. Did she still value his present to her, in remembrance of old times ? No ! She valued it so little that she had evidently forgotten it. Perhaps her maid might have included it among the small articles of luggage when they left home, or dear little Kitty might have put it into one of her mother's trunks. In any case, there it was now, abandoned in the drawer of a table at an hotel.

"Oh," he thought bitterly, "if I could only feel as coldly towards Catherine as she feels towards me!" His resolution had resisted much; but this final trial of his self-control was more than he could sustain. He dropped into a chair—his pride of manhood recoiled from the contemptible weakness of crying—he tried to remember that she had divorced him, and taken his child from him. In vain! in vain! He burst into tears.

CHAPTER XXXVII.

MRS. NORMAN.

WITH a heart lightened by reconciliation (not the first reconciliation unhappily), with hopes revived, and sweet content restored, Sydney's serenity of mind was not quite unruffled. Her thoughts were not dwelling on the evil life which she had honestly deplored, or on the wronged wife to whom she had been eager to make atonement. Where is the woman whose sorrows are not thrown into the shade by the bright renewal of love? The one anxiety that troubled Sydney was caused by remembrance of the letter which she had sent to the convent at Sandyseal.

As her better mind now viewed it, she had doubly injured Herbert—first in distrusting him ; then by appealing from him to the compassion of strangers.

If the reply for which she had rashly asked was waiting for her at that moment— if the mercy of the Mother Superior was ready to comfort and guide her—what return could she make ? how could she excuse herself from accepting what was offered in kindly reply to her own petition? She had placed herself, for all she knew to the contrary, between two alternatives of ingratitude equally unendurable, equally degrading. To feel this was to feel the suspense which, to persons of excitable temperament, is of all trials the hardest to bear. The chambermaid was still in her room—Sydney asked if the post-office was near to the hotel.

The woman smiled, " Everything is near

us, ma'am, in this little place. Can we send to the post-office for you?"

Sydney wrote her initials. " Ask, if you please, for a letter addressed in that way." She handed the memorandum to the chambermaid. " Corresponding with her lover under her husband's nose!" That was how the chambermaid explained it below stairs, when the porter remarked that initials looked mysterious.

The Mother Superior had replied. Sydney trembled as she opened the letter. It began kindly.

" I believe you, my child, and I am anxious to help you. But I cannot correspond with an unknown person. If you decide to reveal yourself, it is only right to add that I have shown your letter to the Reverend Father who, in temporal as in spiritual things, is our counsellor and guide. To him I must refer you, in the first instance·

His wisdom will decide the serious question of receiving you into our Holy Church, and will discover, in due time, if you have a true vocation to a religious life. With the Father's sanction, you may be sure of my affectionate desire to serve you."

Sydney put the letter back in the envelope, feeling gratefully towards the Mother Superior, but determined by the conditions imposed on her to make no further advance towards the Benedictine community.

Even if her motive in writing to the convent had remained unchanged, the allusions to the priest would still have decided her on taking this step. The bare idea of opening her inmost heart, and telling her saddest secrets, to a man, and that man a stranger, was too repellent to be entertained for a moment. In a few lines of reply, gratefully and respectfully written, she thanked the Mother Superior, and withdrew from the correspondence.

The letter having been closed, and posted in the hotel box, she returned to the sitting-room, free from the one doubt that had troubled her; eager to show Herbert how truly she believed in him, how hopefully she looked to the future.

With a happy smile on her lips she opened the door. She was on the point of asking him playfully if he had felt surprised at her long absence—when the sight that met her eyes turned her cold with terror in an instant.

His arms were stretched out on the table; his head was laid on them; despair confessed itself in his attitude; grief spoke in the deep sobbing breaths that shook him. Love and compassion restored Sydney's courage; she advanced to raise him in her arms—and stopped once more. The book on the table caught her eye. He was still unconscious of her presence; she ventured to open it. She read the inscription—looked at him—looked back at the writing—and knew the truth at last.

The rigour of the torture that she suffered paralysed all outward expression of pain. Quietly she put the book back on the table. Quietly she touched him, and called him by his name.

He started and looked up; he made an attempt to speak to her in his customary tone. " I didn't hear you come in," he said.

She pointed to the book, without the slightest change in her face or her manner.

" I have read the inscription to your wife," she answered; " I have seen you while you thought you were alone; the mercy which has so long kept the truth from me is mercy wasted now. Your bonds are broken, Herbert. You are a free man."

He affected not to have understood her. She let him try to persuade her of it, and made no reply. He declared, honestly declared, that what she had said distressed him. She listened in submissive silence. He took her hand, and kissed it. She let him kiss it, and let him drop it at her side. She frightened him ; he began to fear for her reason. There was silence—long, horrid, hopeless silence.

She had left the door of the room open. One of the servants of the hotel appeared outside in the passage. He spoke to some person behind him. " Perhaps the book has been left in here," he suggested. A gentle voice answered : " I hope the lady and gentleman will excuse me, if I ask leave to look for my book." She stepped into the room to make her apologies.

Herbert Linley and Sydney Westerfield looked at the woman whom they had outraged. The woman whom they had outraged paused, and looked back at them.

The hotel servant was surprised at their not speaking to each other. He was a stupid man ; he thought the gentlefolks were strangely unlike gentlefolks in general; they seemed not to know what to say. Herbert happened to be standing nearest to him: he felt that it would be civil to the gentleman to offer a word of explanation.

" The lady had these rooms, sir. She has come back from the station to look for a book that has been left behind."

Herbert signed to him to go. As the man turned to obey, he drew back. Sydney had moved to the door before him, to leave the room. Herbert refused to permit it. " Stay here," he said to her gently; " this room is yours."

Sydney hesitated. Herbert addressed her again. He pointed to his divorced wife.

" You see how that lady is looking at you," he said; " I beg that you will not submit to insult from anybody."

Sydney obeyed him : she returned to the room.

Catherine's voice was heard for the first time. She addressed herself to Sydney with a quiet dignity—far removed from anger, farther removed still from contempt.

" You were about to leave the room," she said. " I notice—as an act of justice to *you*—that my presence arouses some sense of shame."

Herbert turned to Sydney : trying to recover herself, she stood near the table. " Give me the book," he said ; " the sooner this comes to an end the better for her, the better for us." Sydney gave him the book. With a visible effort, he matched Catherine's self-control : after all, she had remembered his gift ! He offered the book to her.

She still kept her eyes fixed on Sydney— still spoke to Sydney.

"Tell him," she said, "that I refuse to receive the book."

Sydney attempted to obey. At the first words she uttered, Herbert checked her once more.

"I have begged you already not to submit to insult." He turned to Catherine. "The book is yours, Madam. Why do you refuse to take it?"

She looked at him for the first time. A proud sense of wrong flashed at him its keenly felt indignation in her first glance. "Your hands and her hands have touched it," she answered. "I leave it to *you* and to *her*."

Those words stung him. "Contempt," he said, "is bitter indeed on your lips."

"Do you presume to resent my contempt?"

"I forbid you to insult Miss Westerfield." With that reply, he turned to Sydney. "You shall not suffer while I can prevent it," he said tenderly, and approached to put his arm round her. She looked at Catherine, and drew back from his embrace, gently repelling him by a gesture.

Catherine felt and respected the true delicacy, the true penitence, expressed in that action. She advanced to Sydney. "Miss Westerfield," she said, "I will take the book—from you."

Sydney gave back the book without a word: in her position silence was the truest gratitude. Quietly and firmly Catherine removed the blank leaf on which Herbert had written, and laid it before him on the table. "I return your inscription. It means nothing now." Those words were steadily pronounced; not the slightest appearance of temper accompanied them. She moved slowly to the door, and looked back at Sydney. "Make some allowance for what I have suffered," she said gently. "If I have wounded you, I regret it." The faint sound of her dress on the carpet was heard in the perfect stillness, and lost again. They saw her no more.

Herbert approached Sydney. It was a moment when he was bound to assure her of his sympathy. He felt for her. In his inmost heart he felt for her. As he drew nearer, he saw tears in her eyes; but they seemed to have risen without her knowledge. Hardly conscious of his presence, she stood before him—lost in thought.

He endeavoured to rouse her. "Did I protect you from insult?" he asked.

She said absently: "Yes!"

"Will you do as I do, dear? Will you try to forget?"

She said: "I will try to atone," and

moved towards the door of her room. The reply surprised him; but it was no time then to ask for an explanation.

" Would you like to lie down, Sydney, and rest?"

" Yes."

She took his arm. He led her to the door of her room. " Is there anything else I can do for you?" he asked.

" Nothing, thank you."

She closed the door—and abruptly opened it again. " One thing more," she said. " Kiss me."

He kissed her tenderly. Returning to the sitting-room, he looked back across the passage. Her door was shut.

His head was heavy; his mind felt confused. He threw himself on the sofa— utterly exhausted by the ordeal through which he had passed. In grief, in fear, in pain, the time still comes when Nature claims her rights. The wretched worn-out man fell into a restless sleep. He was awakened by the waiter, laying the cloth for dinner. "It's just ready, sir," the servant announced; "shall I knock at the lady's door?"

Herbert got up and went to her room.

He entered softly, fearing to disturb her if she too had slept. No sign of her was to be seen. She had evidently not rested on her bed. A morsel of paper lay on the smooth coverlet. There was only a line written on it: "You may yet be happy— and it may perhaps be my doing."

He stood, looking at that last line of her writing, in the empty room. His despair and his submission spoke in the only words that escaped him:

"I have deserved it!"

END OF VOL. II.

BILLING & SONS, PRINTERS, GUILDFORD